The Melon Hound

The Melon Hound

by Sandy Dengler

Moody Press
Chicago

© 1980 by
THE MOODY BIBLE INSTITUTE
OF CHICAGO

All rights reserved.

ISBN: 0-8024-5239-6

1

The Emerald Stickpin

"Happy birthday! Happy birthday!"

Daniel sat bolt upright in his bed. Six-year-old Rachel and four-year-old Naomi were shrieking it. Grace, eleven, was snapping it out authoritatively. And Pop and Mom truly seemed happy.

Daniel grinned. "It is! I almost forgot!"

Naomi bounced up and down. "I get to help Mommy bake the cake!"

"Oh, help us all!" Daniel laughed.

"And Grace and I are doing your chores today. All of them. You don't have to do a thing." There was a little twinge of jealousy in Rachel's voice. Obviously, that chore business had not been her idea.

"You mean I don't have to do a lick of work all day?"

"Nope," said Pop. "Go fishing, take a nap—anything your little old thirteen-year-old heart desires."

The thought was dizzying. Anything he wanted to do and all day to do it. No work, no chores, no errands. His family sifted away, some here and some there. Daniel stretched out again. He could go back to sleep, even— just roll over and doze off for another hour or two. But that would not work. He was wide awake now.

Daniel took his time getting into his clothes. He ambled downstairs to breakfast in no haste at all. What a luxurious feeling! Mom broke two eggs onto the griddle as he sat down at the table.

Daniel glanced out the window into the back yard. "Where's Pop going?"

"Pick up Mr. Carson. Then they're driving over toward Joslin to meet a fellow named Devlin."

"Oh."

"Want to go with him?"

"Guess not." It all sounded boring— certainly no way to spend a fine day off.

"Figured out what you're going to do with the day yet?"

"Not yet. Still working on it." He would not have admitted it, but the day itself was beginning to look a bit boring. He could go see Chet, but Chet had plenty to do this time of year. Matt and Carrie were both working today, too. Besides, Carrie would just make a big fuss over Daniel's birthday—maybe she would even get him something. And then he would have to give her something in return, because her thir-teenth birthday was just three weeks after his.

He remembered the leisurely jaunts he had taken when he had Isobel, his javelina*. But she belonged to Chet now. Besides, she was consistently bad-tempered anymore.

And Bess. How he missed Brown Bess! She had been such a good dog and a good friend, too. He would love to go out walking with her now. But she was gone, gathered to her doggy people, to paraphrase the Scripture. *Do animals go to heaven like people do?* Daniel wondered. If any animal deserved heaven, it was Brown Bess.

When Daniel had finished breakfast and found his fishing pole, he still had not decided exactly what to do.

Because Pop had just driven off with both horses, there was nothing to ride on. So he would start by walking down to the river. As he passed the barn, Grace was mucking out the lean-to where the goat lived. Daniel's job normally.

"Thanks, Grace. I really do appreciate this."

"You're welcome. Happy birthday." Grace could be sweet when she really wanted to.

The river was low—very low. Back East, where rivers were wide and grand, this river would not be more than a dinky creek. But the Rio Grande, small as it was, was one of the

---

*Hah-va-LEE-na. A peccary, or wild pig.

biggest rivers out West. Daniel fished a few holes, but most places he could walk to Mexico without getting his knees wet.

Why not? he thought suddenly. *Why not go to Mexico?* Here he had been living along the Rio Grande for over two years, and he had never once set foot in Mexico. In fact, he had heard about some village not three hours' walk distant. By hustling he could get there in two hours, explore around, and still be home in good time. Delighted with his idea, he tucked his pole away under the roots of his favorite sycamore, waded across a shallow riffle, and entered a foreign country.

Mexico did not look a mite different from West Texas. The dirt was just as warm under his feet, the sun just as bright, the dust just as penetrating. The same brush and cactus studded rocky, rolling hills.

Daniel followed the river a short distance and turned south, up over a low ridge. There must be a trail around. Finally he came to a faint track. Burros had followed it recently, and he saw the mark of a sandal. This must be it!

He pressed on an hour more. The track joined a ragged little trail that opened onto a narrow road. Now he was really on the way. From beyond the breast of the hill ahead he heard angry voices approaching. Why ask for trouble? Let the argument pass by. He stepped behind a boulder and crouched down.

The voices spoke Spanish, of course. And

8

Daniel knew only a dozen words of Spanish. He peeked out.

A wagon drawn by two mules approached. Beside it, a tall gentleman with a thin moustache rode a bay horse. The wagoner and the gentleman were arguing violently and shaking fists at each other. Daniel ducked down again. The harness rattled and creaked. Then the wagon stopped—right in front of Daniel's hiding place.

Next Daniel heard a terrible tussle. The wagon jiggled; its springs squeaked. A bright knife plopped in the dust beside Daniel. The horse squealed and backed into Daniel's rock. Then a hand came into sight, grabbing for the knife. It almost grabbed Daniel's foot! He could hear grunting, pounding.

Suddenly the wagoner ran down the road the way his wagon had come. He paused at the breast of the hill to shake his fist again. He shouted something ending in *"por Dios!"* Daniel knew those words. "For God." The man was calling out to God. Then he was gone.

The man with the pencil moustache quickly mounted and grabbed the near mule's bit. He dragged, shouted, and urged the mules to a noisy jog up the road.

Daniel had had enough of Mexico. At least in Texas if he came upon a fight he could understand the language enough to know which side to be on. He started up the road. Ouch! This was no time to get stuck with a thorn.

But it was no thorn. It sparkled. Daniel picked it up. It was a gold stickpin. The head was a brilliant circle of dancing diamonds surrounding a lovely green stone. Green. Emerald. Had one of the fighters dropped it, or had it lain here for months? Well, no finding the owner now, even if he could speak some Spanish. Whoever saw it would claim it, whether it was his or not. Daniel thought a few moments. Then he tucked the stickpin deep in his good pocket.

He arrived back at his fishing pole by 11:00 AM.

When Daniel got home, Mom was finishing lunch and the girls were out hanging up wash. Mom dished him up a plate of beans and cornbread, refilled her teacup, and sat down across from him.

"Mom, we oughta learn Spanish. I mean, here we are sitting right on top of Mexico. Think we could?"

"Possibly. You didn't ask this morning who Mr. Devlin is."

"All right. Who's Mr. Devlin?"

"A schoolmaster, working at a store in Joslin. Your father and Mr. Carson went out to talk to him about coming here."

"You mean Springer?"

"Springer has a school. Here on the river-bottom."

Daniel counted on his fingers. "Let's see. There's me and Rachel and Grace, three. Cliff,

Matt, and Carrie, six."

"And the Guirran boys. Nine."

"And Chet, Margaret, and Barton. Twelve."

"I doubt anyone will talk Chet into going to school. Margaret might catch herself up. And Barton for sure."

"And Hawes. Melanie and Marianna. Mom, I know what! The Guirran boys. They don't speak English much. We can help them in English, and they can teach us Spanish!"

"Wonderful idea, Dan."

"I'll go over to Guirran's this afternoon."

"Now hold on. We don't have the school yet. It's still talk. We may not be able to pay him enough. There's only five families, you know."

"And things are kinda lean, aren't they?"

"Absolutely gaunt." Mom drained her tea and stood up. "It may be your birthday, but it's not mine. I have work to do. Enjoy your day off, birthday boy." She kissed Daniel on the forehead and went outside.

Daniel liked it when she did that, but not if someone was watching. And lately she never did if others were around. Daniel appreciated that.

Daniel climbed to the loft and stretched out on his bed. He examined the stickpin more closely in the half-light. It was gorgeous. And Christmas three months away—that was it! Daniel would give it to Mom for Christmas. What a surprise that would be. He supposed he ought to tell Pop about it, though. First chance

11

he got when they were alone, he would tell Pop. He put the stickpin in a sock and rolled the pair up into a ball. He tucked the socks away. As long as they were clean Mom would not bother them.

That bit of thinking was satisfactorily completed. But Daniel still had the rest of the afternoon. Good a time as any to catch up his Bible reading. One of the things Matt Carson had said that first hour of Daniel's new life in Jesus Christ was that Daniel ought read his Bible every day—at least three chapters.

Let's see. He had been a Christian two weeks now. Three times fourteen days was forty-two. He should be in Matthew 42. Only twenty-seven chapters in Matthew though. So he should be fifteen chapters into Mark. He should be nearly done with Mark, and he was only on chapter 7 of Matthew! Well, he would not get caught up today, but he could get a good start. He tucked his pillow against the headboard and settled in.

"Not everyone that saith unto me, Lord, Lord, shall enter into the kingdom of heaven; but he that doeth the will of my Father which is in heaven."

Could that be the evil-looking wagoner? He had called to God, but he certainly did not seem to be pursuing a Christlike life. Daniel must be careful not to fall into that trap himself—saying, "Lord, Lord," but ignoring what Jesus wanted. He was just starting to read the account of the Gergesene demoniacs when he fell asleep.

That night at supper Pop announced that Mr. Devlin had accepted the teaching position. After two years without schooling, Daniel and his sisters would again be pupils. Grace cheered. Rachel chewed her lip—she had never been to school. Daniel enjoyed school, but he certainly was not going to say so out loud.

After supper the girls cleared the table, and Pop hauled out three newspapers Mr. Devlin had given him. One was only a week old. Mom and Pop sat at tea and read papers, so Daniel poured himself some tea—with lots of goat's milk—and read papers, too. After all, his birthday was not over yet.

In fact, calculating his chances, Daniel casually put his feet up on the table and stretched out with a paper. Not at all casually, Pop knocked them off the table. He did not have to say anything. Daniel knew. There are certain lines drawn even on birthdays.

Pop shook out his paper. "Now here's history, Dan, or it will be from now on. You recall President Garfield was shot last July and lingering? Well, he died, the nineteenth of this month."

Daniel counted. "Eleven days ago. Does it say if he was a Christian?"

"Says he was a lay reader with the Disciples of Christ church."

"Hm." Daniel nodded. "Course, like Matt says, just because you go to church a lot doesn't guarantee you're a Christian. Lotsa people in churches who don't know Jesus."

Mom cleared her throat in an embarrassed way. "Well, look at this interesting item. 'Border officials'—I suppose that's rurales and Texas Rangers—'are asking everyone to keep an eye out for suspicious persons.' Says someone robbed some high politico in Mexico City and the loot might be coming north our way."

"What loot?"

"Doesn't say, exactly. Permanent settings, apparently. Jewelry that once belonged to Carlota and Maximilian."

Daniel swallowed hard. "Diamonds?"

"Yes, as a matter of fact. Diamonds and emerald pieces, it says."

"Necklaces and brooches and stickpins and stuff."

"I suppose so."

"Yep." Pop nodded. "First place I'd look for precious gems—right here along the riverbottom. Jewels just lying around in the dust waiting to be picked up."

Daniel swallowed harder.

Mom snickered. "Well, don't pick them up, Ira. Those aren't jewels. They're scorpions and cactus."

"Don't speak too lowly of cactus, Martha. You may spend the winter eating it."

"Oh, I don't know. There's quite a reward for

14

information leading to recovery of the jewels."

"How much reward?" Daniel blurted.

"Doesn't say. You planning to become a detective?"

Daniel shrugged. "Bet it would pay better than farming."

Pop grunted, "Lying in bed pays better than farming."

Silence.

Daniel stared at his paper and turned a page occasionally. But he might as well be holding it upside down. Could that stickpin be part of the Carlota jewels? If he told anyone what he knew—which was essentially nothing— someone would take away the stickpin and he would have nothing at all. Besides, whatever he knew could not be considered helpful information.

Daniel tried to picture what Jesus would do. He could not even picture Jesus being interested in any emerald stickpin. What had those men been arguing about so violently? And were they connected to the stickpin any way at all?

Daniel surely wished he knew Spanish.

2

Schoolmaster
Devlin

School. After two years of studying under
Mom at the kitchen table, Daniel would be in
school. A week before it opened, the five
families spent a day putting the school in order.

The schoolhouse and teacher's house were a
pair of abandoned adobes near the crossroads
of the Springer and Tornillo roads. It was
equally distant from just about everybody but
the Guirrans. They lived farthest, but the three
boys were all fine riders. "No matter at all,"
said Don Ramón. "My boys have fine horses."

It was true. The Guirrans were, in fact, well
to do. Don Ramón hired seven vaqueros,* and
his wife had a maid. Their beef cattle were better than Wesmorton's. They even had fancy
Nubian goats, purchased when Pato was a
baby because cow's milk made him sick.

---

*Vah KAY ro, a cowboy, cowhand. From *vaca*,
"cow."

17

The eldest was Ramón. Since he was Ramón Guirran number two, everyone called him "Dos." He had his father's square shoulders, but not the moustache. Not yet. The middle Guirran, Arturo, looked like a scraggly bush. His hair jumped out of his scalp in all directions, and he was lanky—all arms and legs and fingers. He could climb anything in the world, and Daniel envied that. When the rope got stuck in the pulley of the new flagpole, it was Arturo who scurried up the pole, monkeylike, and freed it.

Just the opposite was chubby little Pato. He was six, but he was shorter than Royal Carson who was only five. He was wider, too. Daniel never ceased to marvel how three brothers could be so totally different.

Everyone contributed to the new school. The Guirrans provided poles and built corrals. The women made curtains. The men built benches. The children raked and whitewashed.

No one expected much from the Hollises. But when Chet and Barton drove up that afternoon, their wagon was piled with slate for blackboards and desk slates. They had spent several days driving from town to town, visiting hotels and pool halls to salvage broken slate from pool tables.

Daniel got stuck with the whitewash brush, but Matt was permitted to help the Guirrans. Daniel soon saw why—Matt could speak Spanish almost as well as they. It was not

Christian to envy, but Daniel admired Matt's way with words.

"School" seemed so vague and distant, but suddenly it was the first day. After long freedom, Daniel was seated on a rough bench with Rachel beside him in the close little room.

The Guirrans had arrived, as expected, on their elegant Barb horses. Daniel did not have an elegant horse to ride. But on the other hand, he did not have to wear ruffles, either. El Don Ramón was never without his white ruffled shirt and snug black jacket. On him such dress was natural and proper. Dos looked just as natural in ruffles. But on Pato they were funny and on Arturo grotesque. He was not a ruffled-shirt person. *Did their mother wear ruffles?* Daniel wondered.

The room fell silent, and Daniel turned to look toward the door. Mr. Devlin had entered. He strode majestically like an emperor to the front of the room, turned on his heel, and examined his class through wire-rimmed glasses. Rachel pressed closer to Daniel.

Mr. Devlin was a superb study in geometry. His belly was spherical, his jaw square. The lanky arms generated all sorts of interesting angles, and his legs were shaped like parentheses. His long nose would have subscribed perfectly to the Pythagorean theorem. He clasped his hands before him, thumbs thrust upward, his waistcoat thereby describing an area equal to one half the base times the altitude.

His eyes lighted on Carrie. "Rise and give your name."

Carrie stood. "My name is Caroline Carson. Everyone calls me Carrie, sir." She curtsied ever so slightly and sat down.

Mr. Devlin's eye drifted to Daniel. "You?"

Daniel stood up. "Daniel Tremain, sir." He sat down.

Mr. Devlin stared at him a moment and turned to Arturo. "Where is your home?"

Arturo stood up. "My name Arturo Guirran, sir." He made a nod, almost a bow, and sat down.

Mr. Devlin's face turned dark. Daniel went chilly.

"Stand up, Ar-tour-o."

Arturo did so.

"I asked you where you live, young man."

Beside Arturo, Carrie leaned over and whispered, "¿*Donde vives?*"

"Did I address you, Caroline?"

"No, sir." Carrie belatedly remembered to stand up. "The Guirran brothers are having a bit of trouble with English yet. They'll catch on quick enough, I'm sure." She sat down.

Mr. Devlin's voice was icy. "And I suppose you will translate for them in the interim. You! Stand up!"

Dos popped off the bench.

"Your name?"

"Ramón José Mario Guirran y Vargas, *señor, a sus órdenes.*"

"You!" Mr. Devlin thundered.

Pato hopped up as quickly as Dos had, but he was so short he was shorter standing than sitting. "Pato," he whispered.

"Pato? Just Pato?"

Pato glanced back at Dos, terrified.

Dos spoke up. "His name Emilio Ramón José Guirran y Vargas, *señor.* We call him Pato. Pato is a— a—"

Matt stood up. "A duck, sir. When Pato was just learning to walk, apparently he waddled much like a duck."

The little children tittered. Mr. Devlin's scowl deepened. The titter died quickly.

"You three Mexicans. You will go back wherever you came from. This is an American school. When you can speak the king's English you can return and not until then. I am a teacher, not a caretaker for illiterates."

Carrie cried, "You can't just kick them out, sir! They gave so much for this school. They're—"

The storm on Mr. Devlin's face rained over her. She shrank back, silent and shaking.

Arturo looked anxiously at Dos. Dos looked anxiously at Matt. He did not even understand what Mr. Devlin was saying.

Matt spoke softly. *"Los Guirranes no estan permitidos aquí. Tienen que irse."*

"Pero Mateo . . ."

"Busca a mi padre ydile loque pasó."

Suddenly Dos changed from a pupil to a *patrón,* a *Don* like his father. He was eldest. He represented a proud family. His face hardened. He squared his shoulders. His voice was soft, but firm and authoritative. "Arturo, Pato. *Vengan conmigo."* He turned and walked out slowly, with dignity, as his father would have walked. His brothers followed.

Daniel felt sick inside.

"You. Stand."

Matt was standing. "Sir?"

"You have a fair command of Spanish. Where did you learn it?"

"From the Guirrans and from books their father loaned me. They're my friends, sir."

"Your name."

"Matthew Oliver Carson, sir."

"Your planned occupation."

"I'm not certain yet. I hope to enter the ministry of my Lord Jesus Christ."

The storm in Mr. Devlin's face softened. "Indeed. See me at recess. I wish to speak with you."

"Yes, sir." Matt sat down.

The rest of the day was a blur. Daniel remembered Arturo's undisguised panic and Dos's gentle dignity. He noted the oily way Mr. Devlin talked to Matt all day and the shrill voice he used on everyone else. Daniel realized two years was a lot of missed schooling, but Mr. Devlin did not have to put him in the third

22

reader! Marianna Hawes was in third reader, too, and she was only nine.

It was not fair. Nothing about this whole school was fair.

The moment school was out, Daniel rushed to the corral. He jammed the bit in Caesar's mouth, threw his sisters on the rangy horse's back, and swung aboard. He wanted to get out of there. He noticed the Carsons were just as quick to mount Fred.

Less than a mile down the road they met Pop and Mr. Carson. The Guirrans were with them. Pop did not bother to say hello. "'What's going on there, anyway?"

Matt grimaced. "Mr. Devlin doesn't think much of Spanish. Did he know when he came that the Guirrans would be with us?"

Pop and Mr. Carson looked at each other. Pop shook his head. "Can't remember the subject was ever raised. I never thought twice about it, myself. You, Hank?"

Mr. Carson scratched his beard. "Never occurred to me, either. Any ideas, Matt?"

"Find another teacher. He thinks I'm the greatest blessing to the world since Moses, just because I'm thinking of going to seminary. I don't like the way he talks to me, Pa—like some special pet."

"Better'n being on his wrong side."

"I wonder."

Daniel asked, "Why can't you just tell him the Guirrans are part of the deal and he has to take them?"

Pop sighed. "We can't. One of the conditions he insisted on when we hired him is that he would run the school his way without outside interference. He insisted on it."

Mr. Carson snorted. "Never thought we'd need to make an issue of it. Never dreamed of something like this."

"And he's working for low enough pay as it is."

Carrie was near tears. "But they worked so hard, Pa, and did so much—and we can help them."

"I know that. We'll see it's made right by them. Don't know how yet. Let's talk it over after church Sunday."

Pop brightened. "Say! Why don't you Carsons just come on down to our place for dinner? Talk it over across Martha's fried chicken."

Mr. Carson nodded. "Sounds good, Ira. Matt, you explain to the boys we're gonna work on their problem and see that they get a fair shake."

Pop took Rachel over behind him on Cleopatra, and the Tremains rode home together in silence. How could a day that started out so exciting go so wrong? Daniel dreaded tomorrow. He dreaded school. How was he going to stick with this for a whole, endless, bleak winter?

The Guirrans didn't know how lucky they were.

3

The Goatshed Patch-up

When Pop built this house, why had he made the kitchen so big? Daniel had often wondered that. But now, with six Tremains and six Carsons sitting in it, the room seemed woefully small. Every house should have a banquet hall for use when your neighbor's family is as big as yours, and you want to eat Sunday dinner, and it's raining green frogs outside.

Daniel and Matt were sitting on chopping blocks from the woodshed. Royal and Naomi shared the kitchen stool. One side of the table was sitting on the bench from the back porch. But the fanciest dining set in the world does not make a happy meal, and this was a happy meal. Everyone was laughing, joking, and asking for seconds.

Mom's fried chicken disappeared quickly. Even the boiled rutabaga did not last. Then Mom brought out dessert—a birthday cake as big as Daniel's had been, with a candle stuck in the top. Carrie's birthday was tomorrow. Daniel had completely forgotten it.

"Well, Carrie. Make a wish and blow the candle out," her mother urged.

Carrie looked around. "I wish our school year would go smoothly, and we would all learn a lot."

"Carrie!" her mother chided angrily. "You mustn't wish out loud or it won't come true!" She was a lot angrier than Daniel thought the occasion warranted.

"That's what I'm afraid of." Carrie sighed. She took a gulp of air and blew, but it did not take a whole lot of effort to snuff one candle. Everyone clapped and the cake disappeared even faster than the chicken had.

Then came a lull. Pop leaned back and fished around in his coat pockets for his pipe. "Sure do appreciate the Lord's day, Hank. If this were any other day of the week I'd have six different things facing me to do now. Trim a new wagon tongue, nail up some loose boards in the goatshed, mend a leaky place in our bedroom roof—"

"Know just what you mean, Ira. I still don't have that toolshed built. Or the teddin' machine fixed."

Pop nodded. "And then there's the honeydew projects."

"What's that?"

"Why, Hank, you know. The stuff your wife

sets up for you. 'Honey, do this—honey, do that—' "

Mom turned a bit red. "Ira, you know I don't ask anything that isn't necessary."

Everyone was laughing, including the goat.

The goat?!

"That sounds like Granny, and right here in the room!" Daniel exclaimed. He opened the kitchen door.

Granny's coarse tail was flicking back and forth, right in the doorway. Daniel pushed her away and stepped outside.

"Granny, you dolt. Do you realize what your milk's gonna taste like if you eat those rutabaga leavings?" Daniel looped his belt around her neck and dragged her away from the slop pail by the door. She baaaed a protest.

Pop leaned on the doorpost. "Guess I fix the pen Sunday or no. Lock her up in the woodshed for now and let's nail those boards up."

Daniel hauled off the goat, fighting all the way. By the time he got to the barn, Mr. Carson and Pop were already rummaging through the nail keg. Mom and Mrs. Carson were analyzing Granny's escape route. With all those boards loose, Granny pretty much had her choice of exits.

Matt called, "Where's your ladder, Mr. Tremain?"

Pop rubbed his chin and replied, "Well— uh—that's why I haven't fixed that goatshed before now. Need a ladder to get to it, and right now I don't own one. In fact, Martha fried the chicken on the last of the pieces. Weren't worth a whole lot, that ladder."

"Shoulda mentioned it," Mr. Carson said. "Coulda brought mine over."

Mrs. Carson sniffed. "Yours isn't much better. Should be using it in the wood stove, too. You're going to break your neck on it one of these days."

Matt suggested, "Maybe we can pull one of the wagons in close and stand on it."

"Tried that," said Pop. "The hubs hit the adobe and you can't get close enough."

Carrie and Mr. Carson offered some suggestions. Daniel suddenly noticed that Mrs. Carson was still complaining about her husband's ladder, and no one was listening to her.

"We need Arturo Guirran to just climb up the side of the wall." Carrie laughed.

"He could, too, I bet!" Daniel laughed too. "He can climb a greased rope."

Granny was bleating in the woodshed.

"Your goat wants us to hurry up," said Carrie.

Daniel shook his head. "Don't believe nothing she says."

"I got it!" Mr. Carson stood directly below the loose boards. "Matt, Dan, c'mere. Matt, you stand right here. Stoop over. That's it. Dan, you beside him. Brace yourselves 'gainst the wall."

Daniel, stooped over with his head against the wall, tilted slightly to look at Matt. "Does your father always come up with ideas this crazy?"

"Not always. He sleeps about six hours a night."

Mr. Carson planted one booted foot on each boy's back and cautiously stood up. "You boys stand still down there!"

Pop stooped over beside Daniel. "Martha, can you climb up there and help Hank?"

Mom sighed, just a little reluctant. "Guess I've done stupider things in my life. Carrie, you hand me the nails, once I'm up there. She climbed up on Pop's bowed back and stood teetering. "Ira, if you let me fall I won't speak to you for hours. Maybe days."

"Don't tempt me."

Daniel suddenly realized Mrs. Carson was still talking, still complaining, and her voice was even more strident. Instead of excoriating the Carson ladder, she was now begging Mr. Carson to go get it and stop this foolishness. No one paid attention to her.

Mr. Carson's bootheel dug into Daniel's back. Matt yelled at him to quit shifting around. Daniel heard hammer-pounding—two different notes. One note sounded when Mom struck a nail square, a satisfying *quink!* The other was heard when she missed the whole thing and the hammer struck nothing but board, *bunk!* The quinks and the bunks were

29

about equal in frequency.

Pop grunted. This was obviously harder work than he had anticipated. "Martha—quit—trying to be—be ladylike. Just get—get it done."

Matt called, "How're we doing up there?"

" 'Bout got it." Mr. Carson was absolutely cheerful. He could afford to be. He was on top.

More grunts. More shifting of weight. Mom yelped—not a scream, a yelp. The hammer zinged down between Daniel's and Pop's heads and slapped into the dirt. The pyramid was swaying and nobody could save it. The whole human structure collapsed into a tight pile, and Daniel was on the bottom.

He heard Mrs. Carson shrieking. He wished desperately she would be quiet. An impossible weight pressed Daniel's face into the ground. His nose hurt so much that tears sprang to his eyes, but his mouth was mashed too tightly into the dirt to permit him to speak—or breathe, for that matter.

There was much struggling. Elbows, knees, and boot toes gouged into Daniel from several directions. Mom, Carrie, and Mrs. Carson were all offering advice in shrill voices. Then the oppressive weight lifted and strong hands peeled Daniel off the ground. Matt hauled him up, propped him against the goatshed wall, and steadied him a moment until he stood alone.

Matt laughed. "What a mess! I've never seen such a complete mess!"

"Thanks largely, chum. I was hoping you'd tell me that." Daniel touched his sore mouth and sorer nose. Mud. Lots of mud and blood and grit. What about Mom and Pop?

Mom stood nearby, shaking her head and trying without success to wipe the big mud-stains off her apron.

Mrs. Carson grabbed her husband by the shirt and screamed at him, shaking him. If Mom ever tried that on Pop—Daniel could not even imagine Mom doing that. He could not understand Mrs. Carson, either, except that she somehow held her husband responsible. Daniel glanced at Matt and Carrie. Matt was grim and hurting; Carrie was literally embarrassed to tears.

Pop grabbed Mrs. Carson's shoulders, swung her around and squeezed her close. She struggled a moment and melted against him, sobbing. His voice, smooth as oil, was slowly quieting the ripples of her protest.

"Now, Clara, this is *my* house and *my* farm. I don't permit any screaming—not from Martha, not from the kids. You're just gonna have to hold it down until you've left my farm. All right?"

It worked. Mrs. Carson more or less got herself together, and Pop, still talking, transferred her from his long arms to Carrie's gentle ones.

"Carrie, she's to lie down till she feels better."

"Yes, sir." Carrie started with her mother

toward the house. Mom fell in alongside them.

Everyone else stood around in embarrassed silence.

Then Pop spoke. "I apologize for hugging your wife there, Hank. Also for busting my ladder last summer."

Mr. Carson stepped in closer. "Ira, you don't know what a big rabbit you just pulled out of a hat. I can't manage her, and it's getting worse. I don't know what I'm gonna do. She goes to pieces at the least little thing. Then, another day, she'll be right as rain. Think about it. If you can dredge up any advice, give it to me."

Pop turned to Daniel. "Your face looks like forty miles of bad road. Go wash up. Matt, go start some tea or coffee or something."

Daniel poured plenty of water into the basin by the kitchen door, but he did not scrub. He splashed, and very gently. He must indeed have been a mess. The wash water was a terrible color. Mom, all weary, came out the kitchen door. She stopped beside him and tilted his face toward hers.

"You'll live." She walked on out to Pop.

Daniel was grateful she did not make a fuss over him with others watching. He could tell from her eyes she wanted to.

Pop stepped up onto the porch and turned. "Rachel, get Granny out of the woodshed and pen her up where she belongs. The rest of you young'ns find something to do outside here."

"It's all wet out. Can we play in the loft?"

"Go ahead. No fighting. Stack the hay forks in the corner before you start any games." Pop went inside.

Carrie paused in the doorway as Daniel was drying off his face. "Are we young'ns or old'ns?"

"Middle'ns. But I'd rather be in the warm kitchen than out in the cold loft with a bunch of screaming kids."

Carrie nodded. "Let's try for the kitchen. Just pretend you're a mouse in the corner."

They wandered in casually and settled in the corner by the wood stove. Carrie sat on the woodbox and spread out her wet skirts to dry. Daniel hunkered down, leaning against the warm wall. Matt was already pouring tea all around as the grown-ups settled.

Pop leaned back and stretched out. "Sorry Clara got all upset, Hank. I sure do appreciate getting that goatshed nailed back together."

"Glad to do it. Say, heard anything lately on that Charles Guiteau?"

"Nope. But since the president's died, it'll likely go hard on him."

Carrie leaned over to Daniel and whispered, "Who's Charles Whoever?"

Daniel whispered back. "The man who shot President Garfield last July. Mr. Garfield died a couple weeks ago."

Mom was speaking. "Uneducated, as I understand it. Practically illiterate. Now this just goes to show you why our school is so very important. Education is the key to making up-standing, decent citizens." She glanced up. Matt was closest, so she addressed him. "Right, Matt?"

"No, ma'am."

Daniel caught his breath. Matt contradicting his Mom?!

The room seemed to turn cold. So did Mom's voice. "Oh? I thought you were all in favor of education, Matt."

"I am. It's very important. But with all respect, ma'am, it's not the key to making decent citizens."

"What is?"

"Jesus Christ."

"I should have guessed."

Matt continued quickly, "You see, Mrs. Tremain, education can only make a criminal smarter, not better. How many men with university degrees have no moral character, no scruples? Man is essentially sinful, and education can't correct that. But Jesus Christ can. Only through Him can you have victory over sin and the sinful nature. The good citizen is the man who follows Scripture out of love and gratitude for the God who saved him. Man or woman, of course. Women, too."

Mom smiled. "You certainly have Pastor Dougald's line down pat."

"Not his line. God's. Education can't keep you out of hell any more than riches can."

"I trust you don't mean me personally with your 'you.' "

"Yes, ma'am, I do."

Mr. Carson dived in. "Ira, Martha—we been talking about you from time to time. We been worried about you. You're faithful in your church attendance, but, frankly, we don't see the fruits of salvation."

Pop frowned. "Speak plainer, Hank."

But Matt leaned forward. "Many Bible passages call Jesus the bridegroom. And the people saved in His name are His bride. It's just like a marriage. Jesus said, 'I do,' on the cross eighteen hundred years ago. But the bride must also say, 'I do.' You can't belong to Jesus—that is, be saved—unless you actively commit yourself to Him, any more than you can be married without committing yourself to marriage."

"Ira, Martha? Have you two ever deliberately given yourselves over to Jesus Christ?"

Pop was silent, his mouth a thin little line. It was always a thin little line when he was thinking hard and fast.

Mom stammered around. "Well, I suppose—I don't recall exactly—in those words, I mean—"

Matt asked, "Mrs. Tremain, are you certain you are married to this man here?"

"Of course! I should know—" She stopped. "I see. It's that definite, is it?"

Mr. Carson smiled. "You know for sure

35

you're a married woman. You can be that certain about your marriage in heaven, which is your eternal salvation."

Pop glanced over toward Daniel, but he was really talking to Mr. Carson. "And that is what Dan was talking about when he said he'd given his life over to Jesus."

"Yes."

"You're saying he's saved and we're not."

"We're saying he's certain he's saved and you're not certain."

Mom was scowling. "You're telling two churchgoing people that they aren't Christians?"

Mr. Carson shrugged. "There are lots of preachers in the pulpits who aren't Christians. Jesus knew that. He said, 'Many will say didn't I prophesy in your name and do great works? And I will profess to them, I never knew you.' Those people were calling Him Lord and doing many impressive things—even miracles—but they had never committed themselves to Him personally."

Daniel gasped. He had just read that! He had applied it to the Mexican gentleman who had called the Lord's name, but he had never thought to link it to his own parents.

"Ira," said Mr. Carson, "you two are our best and dearest friends. What if we went to our heavenly reward and left you to go to hell just because we were afraid we might hurt your feelings? What kind of friends would we be? We care about you."

"I know that," said Pop softly. He glanced at Mom. She was studying her hands, nervously twining and untwining her fingers.

Pop sighed. "You're right, Hank. Isn't a matter to be guessed at. Well, I know I'm married. Staked down like a tent. I better be that certain I'm bound for heaven. What do we do?"

"Do you two admit to having sinned in your life?"

Mom smiled bleakly. "Maybe once or twice."

Pop added, "Give or take a few thousand times."

Mr. Carson nodded. "Me, too. And it only takes one occasion to break your bond with God. Do you both accept as true the fact that Jesus paid for your sins with His blood?"

"Yes!" They said it together.

"Do you believe Jesus died, was resurrected, and ascended?"

"But we grew up knowing that!" Mom protested.

"I'm talking about really believing it. Accepting it. And will you strive to do God's will as revealed in His Word?"

Pop said, "I do," and laughed. "That does sound a lot like a wedding!"

Then all heads were bowing in prayer. It was a fine opportunity for Daniel to wipe his weepy eyes. The words were different, but the meaning was the same. His parents were making the same commitment now that he had made a month ago at Matt's side by the millpond. Now he was not only son to his parents but brother also, in Jesus. He felt the same heart-singing he had felt weeks ago with Matt.

A round of amens followed the prayer, and now Mr. Carson was explaining how Mom and Pop should turn everything over to God and serve Him first.

Suddenly Mom clapped her hands. "I see! I see! Just what I've thought all along! The one thing I've wanted ever since we came to Texas is a cow. We need a cow so badly. That will be my reward. I'll serve God, and He'll provide us the cow."

"Now hold on, Martha—"

"Jesus said, 'Great shall be thy reward,' didn't He? Well, my reward shall be a cow."

"I don't recall," said Pop dryly, "reading in Scripture where God is promising Martha Tremain any cow."

Mr. Carson bobbled his head sideways. "Martha, it's not like that. You can't just—"

Matt touched his arm. "Wait, Pa. The Lord wants you to serve Him because you love Him, not so you'll get something in return, Mrs. Tremain. He'll give you a cow, but it will be a sign of His love. A sign. Not a reward."

"Now, Matt—" Mr. Carson started.

Matt interrupted. "I feel very strongly about this, Pa. Mrs. Tremain will have her cow, but not as a reward."

Matt was always surprising Dan. How could

38

he be so certain? There was no way Pop could afford a cow, especially not with winter coming on.

Mom's voice softened a little. "Hank, I feel so—so churned up. I hope Christians don't feel like this all the time."

"There's highs and lows, Martha, but always the everlasting arms."

Carrie was tugging at Daniel's sleeve. "Come outside!"

Daniel followed her out onto the porch. The kitchen door slammed shut behind them.

Carrie's eyes were wetter than Daniel's. "I'm a Christian, Dan. I wasn't yesterday, I wasn't five minutes ago, but I am now!"

Daniel grinned. He grabbed her and swung her around close. "You're my sister, Carrie, you realize that? We're in the family of God!"

Suddenly Carrie pushed away, laughing. "Just what you need, Daniel Tremain! Another sister! I hope you don't grump about me the way you grump about your other sisters."

"It works both ways." Daniel laughed. "How much do you need another brother?"

"Forget I mentioned it!" Carrie, still giggling, dug into her apron pocket and shook out her hankie. She dabbed at Daniel's lip a little. "Here. It's bleeding again. I'm so glad your nose isn't as big as Mr. Devlin's. You don't need a hole that deep out by the goatshed."

Then they were laughing again.

It was such a warm, joyous thing, the Carsons' friendship. And now they were all one together. Suddenly it was all blue sky.

Not *all* blue sky.

There was one black, ominous cloud that would not go away. And that cloud was the schoolmaster, Mr. Devlin.

4

Lumpy and Friend

Matt leaned over toward Daniel. "Where are you?"

"Matthew 15—verse 19."

"Good. Now when you read the last half of that chapter, pretend you never heard the story before. Pretend you're one of the people there and you don't know what's going to happen next."

"All right. What *is* gonna happen next?"

Matt grinned. "Read and enjoy." And he went back to his own Bible.

Since both boys felt guilty about not reading Scripture as much as they ought, both had decided to use lunchtime for that purpose. Daily for a week now they had been stretching out under the mesquites by the school. Let the other kids romp and scream. Daniel felt good about his Bible reading.

But Daniel did not read the rest of Matthew 15. Mr. Devlin was swinging his brass bell to reconvene school. School was getting worse. Barton could do no good thing. Daniel was not particularly fond of Barton, but he pitied his predicament. Matt could do no wrong. An enemy did not deserve that, and Daniel felt especially bad for his friend.

Mr. Devlin consistently ignored Carrie and Daniel. Daniel loved the lack of attention at first. But by the end of October he began to feel the loss. Marianna Hawes moved up to fourth reader. Mr. Devlin never bothered to test Daniel's reading. And Daniel knew he could read and spell a lot better than Marianna could.

On the positive side, Mr. Devlin was very good with the little ones. Rachel was all the way up to page 47 in her primer and reading well. Daniel considered talking to Mr. Devlin about moving ahead faster, but no—he remembered something about letting sleeping dogs lie. And from there he thought again about Brown Bess. He missed her. He wished she were back. He wished they had any dog. He really liked dogs. He daydreamed most of the afternoon away thinking about dogs.

He thought of the stickpin, too. He still had not mentioned it to Pop. Maybe he ought to say something about falling behind in school, too.

Pop had both horses, so the pupils walked. They were late getting home, but Mom had fresh cookies and goats' milk waiting.

"How'd it go today?"

Grace shrugged. "Oh, all right."

Rachel filled her mouth with cookie.

42

"Mommy, can we have a baby?"

Mom stopped cold and stared. "Can who have a baby?"

"We'll name it Kate. Can we? Huh?"

"Rachel—"

Daniel laughed. "I get it. There's this story about a baby named Kate in her primer. She just read it today. Don't worry, Mom. She reads about lambs tomorrow. Then she'll want a lamb instead of a baby."

Mom smiled, relieved. "I hope there aren't any elephant stories in your primer, Rachel. First we get a cow. Then lambs."

Wheels rattled outside.

"Oh, there's your father! Set the table, Grace. Daniel, fetch in some firewood."

"That doesn't sound like Pop. Are you sure?" Daniel crossed to the door. "Mom! We got company!"

The stranger standing by the porch wore the dress of a peón*; white cotton shirt and pants, broad, floppy hat. His hair and whiskers were flecked grey—in fact, they were almost the same color as his little grey burro. The burro was attached by an oft-mended harness to a two-wheeled cart with a wicker cover.

Behind the cart a sorry-looking tan cow was tied. A weary hound had already flopped in the dust under the cart axle.

---

*PAY own; a Mexican farmer or sharecropper; a member of the poorer class.

Daniel was taken immediately by the dog. It was a blue-grey with reddish flecks. The skin was several sizes bigger than the dog itself and the ears, long flaps of soft suede leather, drooped from his head down to his ragged paws. This was a hound who had traveled many, many miles.

The gentleman doffed his limp sombrero and swung it in a wide, elegant arc. *"Buenas días, señora muy estimada, y mil flores para usted."*

"Uh, how do you do. What do you want?"

The girls crowded in the doorway, staring.

"I speak husband, pleese?"

"He's not—he'll be home any moment."

"Eh—"

"He will return any moment."

"We sit? Wait?"

The gentleman took a step forward. Mom took a step backward. Without thinking, Daniel moved quickly between them.

Mom cleared her throat. "No, I think you'd better leave and come back some other time."

Obviously, the gentleman had not caught a word of that. He looked perplexed, then quickly covered his confusion with a big smile. Yellow-stained teeth peeked out from under his moustache.

Daniel had started sifting out thoughts as to what he should do next when Pop came rattling into the yard. Caesar and Cleopatra were at a jog, something Pop normally never permitted. Mom radiated relief.

Pop studied the burro cart and took his time climbing off his rig. "Rachel, Grace, go put up the horses."

The girls scowled. That meant missing all that might happen next. But you do not argue with Pop when his voice is that sharp. They tumbled off the porch past Daniel and commenced unharnessing, working as slowly as possible.

Pop stepped up to the gentleman and shook hands. He was head and shoulders the taller. "What can I do you for, sir?"

There was that smile again. "I sell thees cow. Fine cow, no?"

Pop glanced at Mom. Her mouth had dropped open.

"Fine cow, no."

The gentleman trotted quickly to the rear of the cow, reached beneath her, and squirted a stream of white milk into the dust. "Good milk. Much milk. You use good cow, no?"

Mom stared at the brown spot in the dust. Milk. White milk. Cow's milk. A real cow.

Pop pried the cow's mouth open to examine her teeth. Daniel knew you did that with a horse, but a cow—? Pop poked at the numerous warble lumps on her back. He ran his hand down her hind leg.

The gentleman pressed on. "The money. Five dollars?"

Pop shook his head. "Not worth fifty cents." He reached under her distended belly and tugged at the udder. Three of the four were all that were working.

"Tell you what, sir. If you want to get rid of her I'll give you one dollar for her. No more."

"A dollar? One? American? Four. Maybe three. No less."

Pop turned and looked the small gentleman in the eye. "Now see here, sir. I don't even know for a fact that this is your cow, though I admit she matches the rig here. I worked hard today, and I'm not in a haggling mood. I said a dollar. *Uno*. That's it."

"Two. Two, no less."

"One. Adios."

"One. American. Silver, *no papel*."

"One silver dollar and a bill of sale saying she's mine."

"Silver. *No papel*."

Pop sighed. "Martha? Got a silver dollar in the house?"

"Oh, yes! Just a moment." Mom disappeared inside. Daniel heard the cracked teapot rattling. He figured there must be some reason Pop did not send him off with the horses, so he stayed where he was, watching.

Mom came out with a silver dollar, an old envelope, and a pencil stub. "I couldn't find a clean piece of paper. Sorry."

"This'll do." Pop scribbled a few words on the envelope, explained them one at a time to the gentleman, and handed him the pencil.

The stranger hesitated. Obviously, selling a

46

cow was more complicated than he had anticipated. Then he signed the bill of sale with a
tight, trembling script.

Pop handed him the coin and pumped his
hand up and down. "Martha? Do we have a
loaf of bread or something to send along with
this gentleman?"

"If you don't mind biscuits tomorrow."

"Good. Fine."

Mom gave the gentleman a loaf of fresh
bread. She also had some boiled rutabaga and
two chicken wings. The man accepted them
gratefully with much flowery Spanish. Pop un-
tied the cow and handed it off to Daniel. For no
reason Daniel could see, the man then took his
rope and tied it around the dog's neck.

Pop, a hand on the stranger's shoulder, led
man, dog and burro out of the yard and down
the road. After he set them on their way, he
leaned against the corner of the house watching them until they were gone from sight.

When he returned to the cow, Mom was already offering her a warm bran mash. The cow
did not seem particularly interested.

"Well, Martha, Matt said you'd get a cow.
Here she is. Your sign from God."

"You aren't making fun, are you?"

"Fun? Never. Matt said a sign. This poor old
critter can't by any stretch be called a reward.
Sign, yes. Reward, no."

Daniel looked the cow over more closely.

47

The old beast had to be a hundred years old. Her skin was stretched tight over her angular hips, stretched tight over the bulging belly. Her ribs were as sharp as her eye was dull. And the lumps! Daniel had seen various sorts of thoroughpins and bog spavins on horses, but the lumps on the cow's legs defied description. Her back was ripply with numerous hard, round lumps of warble flies. And along her side, down behind the ribs, were two especially painful looking growths. One of them seeped a bit; the other had a bald spot where hair and hide had sloughed away. And yet, in her day, she must have been a very pretty cow, with big brown eyes and graceful horns.

"Dan," said Pop, "got your knife?"

"Right here."

"Martha. How about some soda water?"

"I'll fetch it right out." Mom hurried inside, her skirts rustling.

Grace came running up. "Is this really our new cow?"

"Every bony inch of her. Did you give hay to the horses?"

"Yes, sir. And water. What are you doing?"

"Popping warbles." Pop had flicked Daniel's knife open. Now he was parting the cow's hairs on one of the warble lumps. He chose a place and made a quick slit. The cow barely twitched. Either Pop was a superb surgeon, or she was half numb from old age and starvation.

Pop squeezed and poked. A little worm popped out.

"Oh, gag!" Grace turned her head. Daniel wished she had not done that. Now he was going to prove how strong his own stomach was. But once Pop had extracted several such worms it really did not seem too bad. He showed Daniel how to do it, and they both worked on her. As they worked, Mom bathed the slits with warm soda water. They made a good medical team.

"How about those two lumps on her side, Pop? Gonna open them?"

"They aren't warbles. They could be abscesses of some kind. If I cut them and they accidentally drain into her body cavity, it could kill her. Poison'd spread all through her. We best leave those two, at least for a time."

Mom led the cow to her manger, provided her plenty of clean hay and a big bucket of water, and scratched her behind the horns for several minutes. This was indeed Mom's cow.

Daniel leaned on the stanchion. The cow's mouth was mashing sideways so slowly she might have been chewing in her sleep.

"Why does she eat so slowly?"

Pop leaned on the stanchion beside him. "Probably half starved. Her appetite will pick up quick enough. What's her name going to be, Martha?"

"I don't know yet. I've been trying to think of

something to do with her color or her pretty head."

Rachel pressed against Daniel and peeked between the stanchion boards. "She's lumpy. Even without the worms, she's lumpy."

Daniel shrugged. "There you are, Mom. Call her Lumpy."

Mom snorted. "That's no name for a cow. No dignity. Cows are very dignified animals."

"Sure. Too dumb and too slow to be anything else. You know what the Bible says: a fool sounds like a wise man so long as he keeps his mouth shut."

Mom's hackles were rising. Daniel could feel it.

"Dan, you know you—"

Pop snickered.

"Oh, you two! Come to the house for supper!" She stomped out. From the yard, she called, "Girls! Come help!"

Pop started to move away. Now was probably as good a time as any to tell him about that stickpin. And school. "Pop? Got a minute?"

"Maybe more than one." Pop settled back on the top rail.

"Pop, how did Matt know? He was just as sure as if he'd sold us the cow himself."

Pop shook his head. "Uncanny. Last thing in the world I woulda thought. Bet his pappy is gonna be just as surprised as we are. It's a mystery to me."

"But not to Matt. And speaking of mysteries—"

Rachel burst into the barn. "Mommy says if you expect to eat you better come now. She wants to get supper over with so she can strip her cow. What's stripping her cow?"

Pop swung Rachel up on his shoulders and headed for the door. "You milk her bone dry. Later, Dan?"

"Sure. Later."

They left, and Daniel closed the barn door gently behind him.

Dinner was happy. Mom bubbled as much as Daniel had ever seen her bubble. "You see, Ira? God rewards His own!"

Suddenly Daniel grabbed her arm. "Sssh! Listen!"

Everyone stopped chewing. Pop scowled and shook his head.

"I'm sure I just heard the barn door creak."

Pop dropped his fork and stood up. "Could be our Mexican friend intends to keep his cow and his silver dollar both."

"Ira, be careful."

But Pop apparently did not hear her. He pulled down his dusty shotgun from the top of the cupboard. "Dan, go get the ax out of the woodshed."

"No! He's just a boy!"

"And you and the girls wait right here. I want to know where not to shoot."

Daniel felt excitement boil up inside. He did

not feel scared at all. Not with Pop. He was gone for the ax and back to the porch by the time Pop was out the door.

Pop wiggled his finger and nodded when Daniel understood. They separated. Daniel crossed the yard to the barn by skirting close to the chicken coop. For a panicky second he lost sight of his father. Then he saw Pop darting like a roadrunner from tree to fence to goatshed. Pop flattened his back to the barnside and sidestepped silently to the door. Daniel was amazed at his father's stealth, at the easy way he carried the shotgun.

Of course! His father was a four-year Civil War veteran. He had been only sixteen when he fought in the Battle of Shiloh—only three years older than Daniel was now. No wonder Pop knew his stuff.

Daniel copied Pop's actions as closely as possible, slipping up on the barn from the other side. Pop nodded. Daniel reached out and swung the door open wide. Pop dived in. Daniel heard him roll in the straw. Silence. The seconds crawled. What was happening in there?

From the rear of the barn, Pop called, "Dan. Light a lamp."

Daniel stepped to the door and bolted inside. He flattened out against the inside wall, groped for the lantern, the matches. The first match was damp. It would not strike. The second flared with a startling *fwish*. He touched off the wick and lowered the globe. Nothing moved in his circle of light, including Pop. Where was he?

Cautiously, Daniel crossed the barn floor. Holding the lantern high he peeked into the cow's stall. She had eaten her bran mash and most of her hay. Now she lay on her belly as cows do, her legs neatly folded under. She gazed at him placidly, her jaw working back and forth. She looked like the old men who chewed tobacco on the steps of the courthouse in Springer. Daniel half expected her to spit.

And beside her, curled in an equally neat ball, lay the hound.

"Just the cow here, Pop. And that fellow's dog."

"Reckon the dog came back alone." Pop's voice made him jump. Pop was right behind him. "See how the rope is chewed through at his neck there."

"The cow is his friend, Pop. Look how content he is there. It was him made the door creak."

"No doubt. Might's well leave him here. If he's still around in the morning, I'll take him back to his owner. The burro cart won't have gotten too very far away."

They ambled back to the house, easy and relaxed, so different from the way they had approached the barn.

"Guess Mom doesn't realize what a good soldier you are. She worries too much."

"Just as soon forget it myself." Pop stomped loudly on the porch. He spoke loudly, much louder than needed, "Fetch the ax on inside. We'll put it away tomorrow."

Pop slammed the kitchen door. Daniel stopped at the table, but Pop kept right on going through the house to the front door. "Take just one more little look—" And he was gone again.

Daniel started after him, but his Mom stopped him with a sharp word. She was upset.

Daniel shrugged and flopped down in a chair. "Nothing to worry about. That fellow's dog came back, is all. You should see him, all curled up beside your cow."

Mom was not listening to Daniel. She sat pale and tense, and waited.

It was not until that moment that Daniel thought about praying. He should have been praying for safety since they first heard the barn door. He had forgotten all about God when they needed His support most.

Mom obviously had not thought of Him either. Daniel considered mentioning prayer and decided not to. The idea seemed just a bit embarrassing, somehow. So he offered a silent prayer for Pop's safety and let it go at that.

5

Deals and Bargains

Pop stayed out by the barn an hour, but no one came. Either God was answering Daniel's prayer, or the hound had slipped away from his owner on his own. The next morning the dog was still there with his friend. Mom fed him some scraps and loaded the cow's manger with hay. Then Pop tied a length of clothesline around the dog's neck and rode off with him down the river road.

Daniel and the girls went to school at the regular time. They returned home at the regular time, just five minutes after Pop did and ten minutes before the hound did.

Pop was exasperated. "That brainless old melon hound! Tomorrow you take him back, Dan. I can't lose another day."

"What's a melon hound?" asked Grace. "Is that his color?"

"It's his disposition. He'd rather slink around and suck a melon than stand up and be

55

a good, honest dog. Stuffs his tail between his legs every time you speak to him. Worthless mutt."

The next morning the girls went to school, riding Cleopatra. Mom handed Daniel two apples, a chicken drumstick, and the dog. Pop boosted him aboard Caesar, suggested the Tornillo Creek road, and went off to mend the leak in the bedroom roof.

It would be rainy today. Night rain had wiped out any trace of tracks or prints. Caesar was reluctant to go and kept weaving back and forth across the road, his big, long head over his shoulder half the time. Daniel wearied fast of dragging him around and kicking him. The hound was equally reluctant, always hanging back.

Daniel hated this job. He did not mind missing school, but he surely minded having to return the dog. Pop might call it a melon hound and any other derogatory name, but he was a good dog. He was a pretty dog, too, if you liked big, rangy, freckled hounds. Daniel liked any dog.

By noon Daniel was miles from home and had yet to see any sign of the wicker cart. He spotted a patch of grass by a screwbean and stopped for lunch. Caesar grazed, Daniel bit into his apple, and the dog sat on its haunches and stared at him.

Brown Bess had begged now and then, but she was strictly an amateur compared to this beggar. The hound fixed his eyes on the apple—his big, brown, woeful eyes. He cocked his head.

"You realize what you're begging for, hound? This is an apple. Dogs don't eat apples."

The brown eyes looked even more pitiful.

"All right, but remember. You asked for it."

Daniel bit off a small piece of apple and held it out. The hound's heavy tail thumped the ground. He leaned forward and sniffed. He grabbed it and gulped it down. Again, those big brown eyes, staring at the apple.

"You really are a melon hound!" Daniel finished his apple to the core. The dog ate the core. The dog ate the second core and the skin off the drumstick. Daniel knew better than to feed a dog cooked chicken bones. He buried his bone under a huge rock, where neither wayward hounds nor random coyotes could dig it out.

Did that reward business really work the way Mom thought? After all, they had been going to church for years. And although Pop tended to fall asleep during the sermons, Mom had been listening all those years. Most of the time, at least. She must know a little something about it.

She had made a deal with God and it was working. She had her cow. Might Daniel strike a similar bargain?

"Come here, dog."

The hound moved in closer and plopped

down by Daniel's knee. His tail wagged in quiet, cautious circles. Daniel rubbed him between his front legs—Bess's favorite place. The tail slammed joyfully back and forth. The big, hard hound head burrowed into Daniel's lap.

Let's see. If Daniel might have a dog—this one or another as nice as this—he would—uh—read his Bible every day. He knew God wanted that. He would get caught up, three chapters a day minimum. He would act more Christlike, especially around his sisters. He would not let them get on his nerves so much. And he would help out more around the house.

Daniel felt pleased with the bargain. He hoped God did. Surely God did—it had all the elements God wanted.

And yet, when Daniel swung back up on Caesar and started down the road, he felt silly. God knew they could not afford to feed another mouth all winter, especially a dog, which essentially ate people-food. Perhaps in the future, though, after Daniel had earned his reward by the specified good behavior—

Twenty minutes later Daniel saw the wicker cart far ahead, and his heart fell. He wanted this hound, this lovable old melon hound, not some future dog.

Daniel called out gently as he approached the cart. No one was around. Yes, there he was, over by the rocks. The Mexican gentleman stood up and came over to him.

The gentleman smiled and wagged his head.

"Ah, Your Own. Your Own."

"No, sir, not ours. Yours. We can't afford a dog, not this winter." Daniel stayed aboard Caesar.

"Cow and dog. *Buenos amigos,* eh?"

"Yeah. Inseparable. That's the trouble. But we bought the cow, not the dog."

The man nodded and shrugged. "You take Your Own."

"He's not ours, sir! Pop doesn't want him."

The man smiled with his yellow teeth and took the twine leash. "Your Own stay here. Thank you."

Daniel nodded. "Have a good day, sir." He started to turn Caesar away, but he turned back to the man again.

"Sir? What's the dog's name?"

"Eh?"

"The dog. His name."

"Your Own. His name, Your Own."

"Oh! Now I get it." What a strange name for a dog. Daniel took one last, long look at the hound, wrenched Caesar around and clattered away toward home. He did not want the Mexican gentleman to see the tears in his eyes.

Thursday. And school was miserable. It was not that Daniel missed the dog even more than he thought he would. He made the mistake of mentioning in his absence excuse that the dog belonged to an itinerant Mexican. Mr. Devlin did not believe boys should miss school returning wayward dogs to non-Americans. Daniel was assigned a variety of menial jobs—filling the water bucket, bringing in stove wood, splitting kindling (Mr. Devlin's as well as the school's). That wiped out both recess and lunch hour. He did not get any Bible reading done at all today, and that was the first full day of Daniel's bargain with God.

On the way home he blew up at Rachel for squeezing his waist too tight. Grace picked some silly argument with him, and Mom, at bedtime, chided him for not getting the goatshed mucked out. It was a rotten day all around.

Saturday morning Mom went out to milk her cow and nearly broke a leg stumbling over the dog.

Pop wagged his head, disgusted. Mom tried chasing it off with the broom. It would slink back, a hopeful look on its saggy blue face, its tail between its legs. Pop chased it off by blasting his shotgun into the air. At suppertime it was still there, hanging around the barn with its friend, the cow.

Mom served supper—pot roast and rutabagas—and bemoaned the pigheadedness of some dogs.

Pop mumbled, "Miserable excuse of a mutt would rather pal around with a cow than a human. Stupid."

Grace picked at her rutabaga. She considered herself an expert on animals. "Obviously, his master is mean. And Lumpy is the only friend he has, the only one who loves him for himself."

I love him for himself, thought Daniel, but he did not say that. Instead, he said, "Well, maybe we could let him hang around awhile. We could use a good watchdog."

Pop snorted. "We could use a good watchdog, but that's not him. If someone tried to break in the place here, he'd show 'm how to get the door unlocked. And then serve tea. If I didn't know for sure who the owner is, I'd shoot him."

"How are we going to return him, Pop? Mr. Devlin skinned me alive for missing a day of school. I made a mistake and said the owner's Mexican. I can't take off another day of school."

Mom asked, "What would we feed him?"

"Scraps. Leftovers, You know."

"Dan, *we* eat the leftovers in this house."

Pop sighed. "On the other hand, I don't see what else we can do. Dan and I can't spend time taking him back, the girls certainly aren't going out alone. Maybe we'll let things slide awhile. Maybe that fellow will come back for him."

Daniel's whole chest bubbled over with joy. This striking bargains with God was working! Mom was right. You just tell God what you want and what you will do to get it. And if the deal is agreeable to Him, you've got it! Daniel only wished he had discovered that system years ago.

Tick tock tick—

"Ah-choo!"

Tock tick tock tick—

"Dan? Are you taking cold?"

"No, Ma'am. Don't think so."

Tock tick tock—

The mantel clock had been ticking as long as Daniel could remember, so many years he did not notice it. Except now. Now even the clock seemed to interrupt him. The girls were in bed, and Mom, Pop, and Dan were sitting at the table, around the coal oil lamp, reading.

The Bible seemed to have the same effect on Pop that sermons did—he was dozing in his chair with the big family Bible fallen open across his lap. Mom, across from Daniel, approached Bible reading as she approached everything else—with determination. She seemed to be getting closer and closer to Jesus.

And Daniel was drifting farther and farther away. It had been nearly a week since the dog returned. And Daniel was not keeping his part of the bargain at all.

He had vowed to be better with his sisters. Instead he found himself arguing constantly with Grace, who was a royal pain lately. Naomi was getting on his nerves a lot—as today, when she "borrowed" his knife to dig in the flower beds. His vow to read the Scriptures diligently had fallen through worst of all. Even the clock was distracting him. And as for finishing chores promptly—

"*Aha!*" Mom fairly shrieked it.

Daniel jumped, and Pop sat bolt upright.

"Here it is, right here! I knew it! Listen to this, Ira. Psalm 18: 'The LORD rewarded me according to my righteousness; according to the cleanness of my hands hath He recompensed me. For I have kept the ways of the LORD, and have not wickedly departed from my God. For all his judgments were before me, and I did not put away his statutes from me.' Now listen to this! 'I was also upright before Him, and I kept myself from mine iniquity.' That's sin. '*Therefore* hath the Lord recompensed me according to my righteousness, according to the cleanness of my hands in his eyesight.' Let's see Matt and Hank argue around that. It's right here in the Bible."

Pop smiled. "Show it to 'm Sunday. But I bet they'll have something to say about it. Doubt you can get one up on those two."

"Mom might be right, Pop. I promised God I'd do certain things if I could have a dog."

Mom scowled. "You mean you're responsible for that melon hound hanging around here? Do you know I caught him twice this week chasing chickens? And there's not a rope in the world you can tie him with that he won't chew through. And he knocked Naomi over twice. She won't even go outside if he's not locked up in the woodshed."

"He'd never hurt her, Mom!"

"Not intentionally. But he outweighs her by half. Knocks her down just saying hello."

"I guess he does swarm all over you some. But he'll settle down, Mom, soon as he gets used to us."

"He'd better. And if he gets one of my chickens I'll break his neck." Mom returned to her reading.

Daniel settled back into Matthew, but he could not concentrate. She wouldn't really, would she? He glanced over at her, at the grim determination.

She would.

Early Friday morning she very nearly did. Daniel was out in the corral slipping the bridle over Caesar's ears when the farmyard exploded. The two red hens burst in harried flight toward the woodshed roof, squawking. Naomi was running toward the house, screaming, the chicken feed pan in her hand. And out in the middle, the hound had grabbed Mom's best laying hen by the neck. Amidst a cloud of feathers, the hen was squawking horrendously. Its wings beat wildly.

Daniel skinned between the corral poles and raced across the yard. Mom slammed out the kitchen door with her broom swinging. Daniel reached the hound first. It tried to duck away, but he was quick enough to grab it by the neck. He wrenched the hound's mouth open, and

Mom snatched her blue-speckled hen out of the jaws of death.

"That does it! That *does* it!" Mom was squawking louder than the hen. The hound cringed, its tail between its legs.

Pop came running up. "He get 'r?"

"No. Her feathers saved her. At least, I think she's all right. But she probably won't lay for a week, she's so upset."

Pop turned to Daniel. Daniel felt that if he had a tail it would be between his legs, too. "Well, Dan, I don't know what kind of a deal you made with God. But you're rewriting the contract, and right now. Hank and I are taking those corral poles into Springer. And that hound isn't going to be here when we get back. Not ever. Got me?"

"Yes, sir."

" 'Nough said."

Mom opened her mouth to speak, but Pop looked at her squarely. Enough said. She gathered her speckled laying hen under her arm and went into the house.

Daniel slipped his belt around the dog's neck, a makeshift leash, and wandered off to find some twine. He should have expected this. He certainly had not kept his end of the bargain. God would be the first to point that out. Like Pop said, it is not how hard you try, it is how well you succeed that counts. Daniel had not succeeded a bit with any of the points in his end of the deal.

It would be a big job finding the hound's owner. It would be even harder to communicate to the man that the dog must not return again. But hardest of all would be the fatal consequences if this floppy, lovable hound managed to find his way back home again.

Deals with God were not necessarily the greatest things in the world after all.

6

The Mexican Gentleman's Difficulties

Gloom. The desert had many moods, and Daniel enjoyed most of them. But not gloom. A heavy overcast erased all the shadows and dulled all the colors. The scarp behind McKinny Spring usually sparkled in the morning sun. There was no sunshine now to make the millions of tiny mica crystals gleam. There was no rain, yet the air hung heavy. A few suggestions of low-slung clouds looked like the globs of pie dough Naomi played with while Mom baked—dirty from long kneading by grubby little hands. The sky glowered, pasty thick, gray.

Daniel walked all morning before he crossed paths with another human. Manolo, who worked for Wesmorton, was riding out to the Still Creek line shack. Yes, Manolo knew of the man Daniel was seeking. No, he had not seen him for three days. Someone had mentioned a wicker burro cart over near Cienega Wash. Try out west that way, perhaps. Daniel thanked him and wandered off westward.

At lunchtime Daniel and the hound climbed together to the crest of the scarp. He could see for miles in all directions. And yet, he could see nothing. This was hopeless. There was no way to find one gentle old man in this vast and gloomy desert.

The dog was no help at all. He was, after all, a hound. You would think he could follow a scent trail if only they crossed it. But he trotted alongside Daniel at an easy, sloppy jog, paying no attention at all to the ground beneath them.

Daniel reached down occasionally without thinking to scratch the dog's neck. Maybe Mr. Wesmorton would like to buy a dog. No. Wesmorton's ranch was too close to their own homestead. The dog would be back in a couple of hours. Daniel would just have to take him so far and get him so tired that he would not bother to return.

By late afternoon Daniel had reached Cienega Wash. He was dog tired, but the dog wasn't. Even if Daniel turned back right now it would be past midnight before he reached home. No, later. He would have to wait over an hour for the moon to rise. Daniel flopped down beside a yucca.

The dog nuzzled up against him. Daniel reached out and scratched the floppy ears.

Suddenly the dog sat upright. He hopped to his feet and paced a tight circle, whimpering.

"What is it?" Daniel stood up.

The dog started forward. The twine wrapped around his hand, Daniel followed. He was no longer leading the dog. It was leading him.

There it was, away out there! The burro cart was standing in a clump of dead creosote on the lip of a wash, the burro harnessed into it. Now why would the man park his rig there, of all places?

Daniel called out as he approached.

No answer.

"*Señor?* Hey, *señor?*"

Silence.

The burro shied in the shafts, uneasy. The cart did not move. No wonder. Its wheels were jammed in the dead creosote. But where was the owner? Daniel called again.

Chet had long counseled him to be observant, so Daniel walked a circle around the cart, observing. The tracks showed the burro had crossed the little wash at a dead run and stopped only when the wheels bogged down. But where had he come from? Daniel could see nothing unusual out there and surely no campfire smoke. The wash was part of a broad, sandy floodplain. To the right, a ragged cliff angled off toward the southwest.

"Well, let's go back the way you came." Daniel tied the dog to the cart. It took him five minutes to free the wheels. The little cart was a lot heavier than it looked.

They backtracked across the wash, through the creosote and lechuguilla*. Daniel paused to check the little burro's ankles, but they had not been speared by the sharp spines.

The hound started tugging at his rope and yelping, suddenly excited. Daniel turned him loose. He bounded forward through the chaparral, baying lustily. A faint trail continued straight ahead, along the base of the cliff, but the hound was running to the right, up against the foot of the cliff. It finally started to rain. Big, clumsy drops splattered on Daniel's face. Daniel left the tired little burro where it stood and climbed up toward the cliff, following the dog.

Now the hound was yelping enthusiastically. He ran down to Daniel, nearly knocked him over, and ran back up to the cliff. The dog had found his owner. The gentleman lay up ahead, barely visible inside a deep overhang, almost a cave, among the rocks. He must be taking a nap, Daniel decided—a siesta. But why had the hound not wakened him?

Daniel paused, uncertain as to whether he ought to awaken the gentleman. Then his stomach jumped into his mouth and he moved closer for a better look.

The poor man was a mess. His face and

*Lay chu GEE ya; a low agave plant with stiff, sharp spines on the leaf tips.

head were bloodied, his shirtsleeve torn and bloodsoaked. He breathed in short, painful rasps.

Daniel could not think. For a moment he could not even move. "I'll run get help!" he called. But he did not run for help. Where could he go? There was no homestead, no ranch, not a soul anywhere near. Daniel himself was the only person around. Panic started erasing every thought the moment his brain came up with one.

Daniel looked out across the floodplain he had just crossed, to the bajada, to the mica scarp made distant gray by the rain. He had felt alone before, but never like this. Matt said you are never alone when you have Jesus. But Daniel could not dredge up any feeling of the presence of Jesus now—not the least. He was alone. Besides, what did Jesus know about helping an old man so badly battered?

Well, wait a minute. It was Jesus who told the story of the good Samaritan. Pastor Dougald had discussed about that. First, the good Samaritan had compassion. Then he bound up the man's wounds, pouring on oil and wine. Then he had put the man on his own beast and—

First things first. Daniel glanced back at the man. No change. He ran back down to the burro and led it up into the rocks, close to the overhang. He would probably need things in the cart. He wanted it close at hand.

Compassion. That was not hard. One could not help but feel sorry for a fellow this beat up. Bind the wounds. That would be harder. With what? And water. He would need water. Daniel started rummaging, pawing gently through the cart. Its contents were amazingly in order. Things were stacked and tucked firmly so that nothing could shift. The cart was packed. No wonder it was so heavy.

At the back were a goatskin and keg, both for water. The goatskin was empty, the keg nearly so. He would have to go easy on the water. But, look! The stuff was falling out of the sky. And here was a canvas tarpaulin folded up near the back of the cart. A rain apron.

It took only a minute to spread the tarp out across sloping rocks and set the keg near its low edge. Now all the rain falling on the tarp would run off into the keg. It would not refill the keg completely, but every drop would help.

Next, bind the wounds. Bandages. Daniel decided to skip the oil and wine part. That was confusing anyway. There were no sheets or rags that Daniel could find, but here was a white shirt worn through at the elbows. That would have to do. And here were the gentleman's kitchen utensils, all neatly stacked—a bowl, a pan, a pot, and a cup, all tin. Daniel set the pot under a natural pour-off place at the edge of the overhang. More water.

The whole good Samaritan thing took a lot longer than Daniel would have thought. The gentleman half waked a couple times, mumbled in Spanish, and slipped back. Perhaps the man's attackers had used a knife, or perhaps the man was simply trying to fight them off. But the gash in his arm was obviously the result of a blade. Daniel was proud of the job he did on that. He even managed the fancy spiral reverse bandage his mother had taught him last year when Grace cut her shin. Nice work! Daniel was beginning to feel like a doctor.

He wiped the blood off the gentleman's face and rubbed it out of his hair. He wrapped the man in the only blanket he could find. He unharnessed the burro and tethered it nearby. He built a fire, gathered in a lot of extra firewood, and emptied the pot into the keg. He sat down by the man to contemplate supper.

And Daniel's confidence faltered. He did not know the first thing about cooking. In fact, in his rummaging he had not even noticed anything that looked like food. The man had corn flour for tortillas, no doubt, and probably beans, but what did one do with them? The gentleman would not be feeling hungry, but Daniel surely did. The dog surely did, too.

Darkness came and Daniel did not feel so alone. Outside was a black wall of nothing but rustling rain. The fire made the little cave cozy, light, and fairly warm. The gentleman was breathing much easier now—more like a normal person. Daniel remembered how Rachel had suffered with pneumonia in Illinois, and he pushed sand under the gentleman's shoulders and head to raise him up a bit. The dog made the cave seem even homier by curling up at Daniel's feet and snoring.

He had managed. At least he was managing so far. Daniel felt downright smug. With Jesus' help? Daniel still could not feel any presence such as Matt suggested. But God's Word had certainly led him. It had washed away the panic and shown Daniel the way to go.

God's Word! Daniel determined to do better with his Bible reading, no longer in order to earn some favor but simply because he wanted to. A knowledge of Scripture was a very good thing to have.

The gentleman woke up late that evening—Daniel guessed around 9:00 or 10:00 PM. He spoke in Spanish, but the only word Daniel could pick out was "*agua*"—"water." The man drained three cups of water, so that must have been it. Daniel rolled the man's other pair of pants into a sort of pillow for his head. The gentleman lay there many minutes watching him. He studied him so intently that Daniel would have moved somewhere else to sit, had there been anywhere else.

"Uh, sir? Want another cup of water?"

"No. No, *gracias. Basta.*"

"Warm enough?"

"Eh?"

"Uh—cally enty?"

"Oh. *Es bueno. Gracias.*"

"Hey—uh—who did this to you? Do you know?"

"Who?"

"Who." Daniel slammed his fist into his palm. "Who?"

"No sé. Don' know who."

"Why? Do you know why?"

"Why. *No sé.* Don' know why."

"Well, did they rob you? Take stuff?"

"Don' know."

"Oh." Daniel shrugged. So much for that conversation. He watched the fire squirm about on the red coals.

The burro moved from blackness into the outer ring of light. It nibbled at the shrubs here and there and shook itself.

The man spoke suddenly. "You are good friend. A good man."

Daniel laughed. "I'm not a man. I'm just a—"

"No! Not a *muchacho.* A man!" The gentleman patted his sore arm. *"¡Mira!"* He waved his good arm toward the burro, the fire. *"¡Mira!* A good man. A good friend. *¡Dios te bendiga!"*

"Uh, thank you."

The gentleman cleared his throat.

"Here I go along, eh? Three men. We stop. *'¿Dónde 'stá la vaca,* eh?' They want—the cow. 'A man buy the cow.' *'¿Dónde 'stá la vaca?' 'No sé.* Don' know.' Three men, they—"

The man beat himself on the chest with his good hand.

"They beat you up trying to get the *cow*?"

"*¡Sí!* Yes. They say, 'Aaaaah!.' " He waved his good arm, and the burro raised its head in the gloom. "Burro run."

"Yeah, he ran over a quarter mile until the cart hung up in some brush. Why did they want the cow? It's not even a good cow. Mom doesn't get but a quart of milk or so."

"*No sé.* Don' know. They want the cow. They—how?"

"Beat you up?"

"*Sí.* Beed op. I don' know."

"Do they know where you sold her?"

"Eh?"

"Maybe they went to my house. Cause trouble at my house. My *casa.* Trouble."

"Oh. No. No, I don' say cow is there."

"Oh. Good. Still—" Daniel was worried now. But there was nothing he could do. He certainly could not get home ahead of the man's attackers, even if he left right now. But he had better start home as soon as he could. First thing tomorrow, if possible.

But then, the good Samaritan had taken the victim on his own beast to an inn—the nearest place, presumably. It would take days to move this man anywhere. Life was very difficult.

Silence.

"Why do you call your dog 'Your Own'?"

"Your Own?" The gentleman chuckled.

76

"Busca'l libro."

"The what?"

"El libro. El diccionario." He waved toward the cart.

"A dictionary?" Daniel got up and groped through the back of the cart in the darkness. The rain made the back of his shirt damp.

"a la isquierda."

Finally, against the left sideboards, Daniel felt an oilskin bundle that seemed to be books. He dug the parcel loose, brought it over by the fire, and sat beside the gentleman.

He was amazed. He and Pop had both assumed this man was just another peon who could neither read nor write. But the gentleman was much more. Besides the Spanish-English dictionary, he owned a well-used copy of *Don Quixote,* two small volumes whose titles Daniel could not read, and a Bible. *Santa Biblia.* Holy Bible.

Daniel handed the dictionary to the man and leafed through the Bible. It looked so familiar, all set out in chapters and verses. And yet there was not a word there that Daniel understood. That reminded him of Matt's saying the Bible is a closed book to those who do not know Jesus Christ. Words were neatly printed, but the meanings were locked away.

The man's hands trembled as he thumbed through his dictionary. "Here. *Aquí."* He thumped with his finger.

Daniel read the word. *Llorón.* "Lore-on?"

"Yo-*roan*. Say. Yo-roan."

Daniel grinned. "Llorón. So that's how you pronounce it and spell it. I thought 'Your Own' was a little strange. And it means someone who whines. A crybaby. Perfect! Perfect name!"

The man was thumbing through again. He tapped his finger on another page. "Here. *Dios te bendiga.*"

Daniel craned his neck. " 'God bless you.' Thank you. You, too."

The gentleman scooped the Bible over into his lap and started leafing through that. It took him longer this time. But then, Bible phrases were not alphabetical. He found his place in what was obviously Luke.

"Here. This are you."

From a few rather English-looking words Daniel could make out that this was the story of the good Samaritan. He took the Bible into his own lap and worked on the passage a long time, trying to piece together words and familiar phrases. When he glanced up, the gentleman had fallen asleep.

Not a bad idea. He piled wood on the fire, banked sand up behind it, and fell asleep himself.

Something smelled good. Any food would smell good right now, but this smelled especially good. Daniel opened his eyes. The sun was already up. And the sky was clear. The fire crackled. The gentleman's blanket was now lying over Daniel's shoulders. The man himself was moving about very slowly between cart and fire. He doddered like a ninety-year-old.

He grinned at Daniel. "*¡Buenos días!*"

Daniel sat up and stretched. "Good morning. Hey, do you feel all right?"

"Eh?"

"Feel good? Feel bad?"

"Ah! Feel good. And bad. Most, good. *'Qui 'sta'l desayuno.* Come!"

The man had tossed tea leaves into some hot water. Daniel did not like tea, but he was thirsty enough to drink anything now. He shared the man's cup.

The gentleman laid a fresh tortilla in the tin plate, slopped something brown on it, and sprinkled cheese strips across it.

"*El queso es de Guanajuato. Es queso muy fino.*"

The gentleman handed Daniel the tin plate. He put his own breakfast in the big bowl and settled himself ever so carefully down beside Daniel. He closed his eyes briefly and commenced eating. Obviously, his mouth hurt.

The cheese was delicious. The brown glop was delicious. The tortillas were delicious. The whole morning was delicious! Daniel could go home now without worrying about this gentleman. His good Samaritan task was completed. Everything was bright and rosy.

Or was it?

What would he find when he reached home? He located the word *stay* in the dictionary, made sure the man understood that Llorón was not to follow him again, and started the long journey home.

7

The Milk-Cow Rustlers

The last hour of Daniel's walk home he kept glancing over his shoulder, expecting any moment to see Llorón appear. The dog was gone for good. That was a part of growing up, Pop would say.

Pop. Daniel hurried faster. Was Pop all right? Or did those three men manage somehow to trace the cow to Daniel's farm? Had they found the sorry little cow they wanted so badly?

At last! There was the house just up ahead. Daniel broke into a run. Was he tired! He was not used to covering so much distance. He heard Grace's voice. He realized it was Saturday. No school today.

Mom came around the corner of the house, with Grace right behind her, running to him. Why the big greeting? Her face was all knotted. Something was wrong! Mom grabbed him, wrapped herself around him, and half smothered him. "Oh, praise God, you're safe!"

Grace was shrieking, "They stole the cow, Dan!"

Daniel pushed away. "Those three men! They did find her!"

"They tried to sneak her away, but we saw them. Were they ever mean looking." Grace stopped. "Hey! How did you know?"

"Where's Pop?"

Mom shook her head. She was crying. "He's not back yet."

"Bet he and Mr. Carson are delivering those rails out to some ranch—to whoever bought them."

"I'm sure that's it." But Mom did not sound the least bit sure. "Where have you been, and what took you so long?"

"I'm starved. Find me something to eat, please. I'll explain it. I found that Mexican gentleman, Mom, and you wouldn't believe it. He reads the Bible and—"

But Daniel's tale was drowned out three different ways. It was not until half an hour later, when his sisters finished telling about the cow, that Daniel could resume his story.

Past three o'clock already. Daniel finished his milk and went out to the barn to look around. Mom resumed her vigil for Pop by the front-room window. She looked worn and worried.

Grace tagged along at Daniel's heels. "What do you see, Dan?"

"Tracks."

"I know that. I don't mean that."

"Well, look here. The men were on horseback."

"We already told you that."

"Two horses are shod, one barefoot. They came from the northeast. They let down the rails to get Lumpy out. And here go their tracks out due west. They obviously know where they're going, see? Took off in nearly a straight line."

Grace nodded sagely. "Not very fast, though. Lumpy doesn't move fast. They were pulling on her and still it was slow."

The two of them walked in silence, Daniel watching the tracks ahead. Lumpy dragged her feet here and there. He could have told Grace the cow was being forced along. He looked back. The house was a dark speck behind them. He looked out across the empty desert and thought a long time.

"Grace, I know what I'm gonna do."

"What?"

"If they keep going in this direction, they've passed just a couple miles south of Hollises."

"I thought Hollises was up farther."

"Not if you cut across Tornado Wash by Porksaddle. I can be there in half an hour if I hustle."

"Why do you want to go to Hollises?"

"I'm gonna go get Chet. Together we can track those cow thieves and keep an eye—"

"Mom would never let you!"

"Will you listen? And keep an eye on them until Pop brings help. Chet and I won't try to be heroes. We're just going to watch those fellows. Tell Pop soon as he gets back, all right?"

"But Dan—"

"I don't have a minute to lose, either. Wasted too much time already. You run on back. Chet and I'll leave a broad trail, easy for Pop to follow."

"You mustn't!"

"We'll be careful, I promise. Go on."

Daniel took off across the desert, hopping brush. He had to hurry, to put his plan into action right away, lest he start thinking and become afraid. Tracking cow thieves was dangerous business maybe. He glanced back. Grace was watching. Then she turned and ran toward the house.

Maybe he would be a Texas Ranger when he grew up. It would be a lot more fun than farming. Being a Ranger would be especially interesting if the whole job were as exciting as this was right now.

Twenty feet ahead of Daniel, Chet Hollis rode his sleek little black horse at a prancing walk. Chet watched the ground, glancing ahead, pausing occasionally. He claimed Southern Pacific could not put down tracks any plainer than these. And Chet, nearly seventeen, was the best hunter and tracker

84

around. He should know. His shock of red hair shone in the late afternoon sun.

Daniel gave Chet plenty of room, and not necessarily by choice. Daniel was riding Bird-brain, Barton's horse. The name was apropos. Caesar might be bad about road-weaving, but this lanky sorrel was ridiculous. Daniel had to work constantly just to make the animal go at all. Barton did not have a saddle, either, which made riding the bony horse a very uncomfort-able way to travel.

But Chet and Daniel were hot on the trail of Lumpy and her abductors, and the evening was beautiful.

"Chet, how close you think we are?"

"Real close. Trail's so fresh it smells like bis-cuits."

"Think we'll catch up to them before dark?"

"Prob'ly." Chet stopped his horse, and Daniel pulled up alongside. "Drink, Dan?"

"All right."

Chet carried the canteen, since he had the saddle to hang it on. He passed it over to Daniel. "I'm sure glad you showed up this af-ternoon, Dan. This is a whale of a lot more fun than splitting rails."

"That what you'd be doing if you weren't here?"

"Plus whatever else Pa thought up. I gotta find some line of work besides farming."

"Be a Texas Ranger."

85

Chet laughed. "Dan, they chase me. I don't join them."

"They chase you?"

"They would if they knew."

"Knew what?" Daniel passed the canteen back to Chet.

Chet grinned. "The whiskey stills Pa and me have cooking."

Daniel stared. "You make whiskey?"

Chet took a deep swig from the canteen. "Sure. How else do you make a corn crop into cash?"

"What do you do with it?"

"Sell it. But not in Springer. We take it out of the area. That's even more fun than making it. Sell it to saloons and hotels, get in a first class brawl now and then."

"You call that fun?"

"Ever try it?"

"Don't care to. That stuff isn't Christian, Chet."

Chet laughed. "Neither am I! Matt Carson can have his straight ways. I'm gonna live awhile—I mean, really live. Look how it makes Matt Carson into a tottery little old man, and him not fifteen yet."

"Yeah, but what if—" Daniel had a sudden, ugly thought. "Chet, I hope you aren't thinking of picking a fight with those three cow-snatchers."

"Now would I ever think something like that?"

"I can tell by your face—it's the very thing you're planning!"

"Scared?"

Daniel paused. "Yeah."

"You know, Dan, that's what I like best about you."

"That I'm scared?"

"That when I ask you something I get an honest answer, no matter what. Always. Come on."

Chet nudged Tornado, and they clattered up the hill. Daniel kicked Birdbrain and kicked him harder. Barton's old nag was even lazier and grumpier than Barton was.

They rode in silence. Chet concentrated on the darkening trail, and Daniel was wrapped in the blanket of his own thoughts. When Pastor Dougald preached against the evils of whiskey, gambling, and such, he painted black pictures of unholy sinners—depraved people who prowled city streets somewhere at the dark of the moon. But Chet was so bright and open, so easygoing. Ask him for help or a favor any time—just any time at all—and he would drop everything to come to your aid. The picture did not match up, and Daniel was confused.

Chet dragged Tornado to a halt. The sleek horse danced around. Daniel urged Birdbrain alongside and the sorrel stopped dead, altogether willing to stand still. Chet pointed toward the sun swimming on the horizon. "There they are."

87

Far ahead, out in the middle of a sandy flat, three riders moved toward the west. Lumpy waddled behind, her heavy milk bag swaying.

This vast desert, thousands of square miles, and Chet had gone straight to them. Chet could track a soaring eagle back to the egg it was hatched from!

Chet surveyed the land around. "Now we turn into Indians."

"What?"

"Ever see an Indian?"

"No."

"Right! But you better believe they seen you, and lots of times. We stay out of sight, up along that bajada there. Watch where they camp for the night and move in closer."

"I don't like this."

"Look, we're east of them. In the morning the sun will be behind us—in their eyes if they look our way. We're safe. We might even spot some way to get your cow and sneak off. Maybe tonight even. Where's the moon?"

"Last quarter. We won't have light till late."

"That's right! See? You are getting observant."

Chet led off, circling up onto the slopes of the low hills beside them. He knew what he was doing, so why was Daniel so uneasy? Daniel was beginning to regret the whole undertaking.

Jesus. Daniel suddenly remembered Jesus. He was supposed to be following Jesus' example. That was, in fact, one of his agreements in that ill-fated bargain. What would Jesus do in this situation? Daniel raked his memory for any little guiding fact, any incident. In no way could he picture Jesus out on horseback chasing after some cow, and especially not on a cantankerous old horse like Birdbrain. *What was Daniel doing out here?* He suddenly very much wanted to be home and safe where he belonged.

It was nearly dark before the three riders stopped for the night. They chose for their campsite a small, steep draw, a wrinkle in the smooth skirt of the bajada. One man took up watch at the mouth of the tiny canyon. The others puttered about efficiently, getting comfortable.

Daniel and Chet tied their horses in a creekbed beyond a hill and worked in closer, moving at a crouch from bush to boulder to bush. Daniel admired Chet's cunning. He thought briefly of Pop. Pop was equally good at this sort of thing. The boys settled down where they could see the camp well.

Daniel asked, "Do you think they'll keep a lookout all night?"

"Sure. If I was a cow thief, I would."

"Now we know where they are, let's get back to our horses."

Chet did not move. He seemed to be thinking.

"Chet? Come on."

"They're not gonna stay back there, you know. Oh, they'll camp there. But the only grass is out this way, outside the draw. They'll bring the cow down here, for the grass. And their horses, too, of course."

"Chet! Forget it!"

"And when they bring the animals down they'll picket them. Don't want to hobble them, maybe let them wander off in the dark. And they'll keep a man with them, prob'ly. We have to count on that happening. That means I'd have to sneak in and untie the cow."

"Right under some fellow's nose. Sure."

"Long as I don't stand up, he won't see me. Not in this dark."

"You can't lead a cow away slithering on your belly."

"I know. I know. On the other hand, we might—now what's that?"

Daniel raised his head for a better look. "Llorón!"

"Your own what? Looks like a dog. Hey, that hound you told me about? Hangs around with the cow?"

"Yeah. He must've followed Lumpy out here by scent the whole way. He's a better hound than I thought he was. Chet! Those fellows saw us!"

The three were all standing alert, bristling with rifles and hand guns, looking out towards Chet and Daniel. The boys crouched low.

Chet peeked cautiously. "They didn't see us.

90

They think Llorón is part of whoever might be tracking them down. Just stay low. They'll quit being nervous when they figure out that the dog and cow are amigos."

Daniel lay on the cool stones and closed his eyes. What a mess!

"Dan, do the dog and cow always follow each other around that way?"

"Guess so. They did at our place."

"They are now. One of the fellows is bringing the cow out, staking her out in the grass. And the dog's right with her. Does he come when you call?"

"The dog? Sometimes."

"Spanish or English?"

"Usually won't obey either language."

"We'll chance it. 'Come here' in Spanish is *ven aquí.* Say it."

"*Ven aquí.*"

"Good! Now here's what you do—"

A short time later the boys were in position, ready to put Chet's bold plan to work. Daniel lay on cold, damp gravel, hoping very much the idea would work—and dreadfully afraid that it would not. It was dark now, pitch black. Chet had guessed correctly. One man stood watch, his head partly silhouetted against the blue-black horizon. A second stayed in camp—cooking, probably. The third staked the cow and horses out near the canyon mouth and then settled down beside them. A flicker and then a glowing red dot told Daniel the man

91

had lighted a cigar. Out in the black distance were the munching noises animals make.

One of the horses snorted loudly. No doubt it had detected Chet in the blackness, crawling stealthily in amongst the grazing animals. The horse blew air and rattled stones as it backed off. Would the herder come investigate? Then all was quiet again.

Now Chet would be untying the cow's tether line. He would be but a few feet from the relaxed herder, from that faint red dot.

A poorwill cooed softly a few times and was silent. That was Chet, signaling that the cow was loose. Now came Daniel's part.

Daniel rose up on his knees. No worry that he might be seen. No one could see more than a few feet in this darkness, including Daniel. He threw a chunk of Chet's salt pork toward the grazing animals. He heard it plup softly among them. The horse startled again. A pause.

Daniel threw another chunk, not so far this time. He paused again, counting to twenty. He threw another, closer yet. He heard the unmistakable lip smacking of a hungry dog. It was working.

Daniel flipped a bit of salt pork into the darkness just ahead of him. Here came Llorón. And the cow was wandering along right behind him, looming out of the blackness, snatching grass as she came. Chet was brilliant!

"Ven aquí," Daniel whispered. "Come here,

Llorón." He passed the last bit of salt pork to the dog by hand. He slipped a rope around the cow's neck and moved as silently as he could toward the wash and their horses.

Behind him one of the horses snorted again in the blackness. He must not look back or hesitate. The moon would soon rise, and by then they must be beyond sight of the camp.

Daniel grew impatient. Lumpy, tired and hungry, was in no mood to walk further. Daniel had never realized how slow a cow could be. He reached the horses. So far, so good. He swung aboard Birdbrain and immediately discovered a serious flaw in the plan. He had no saddle, so no saddle horn over which to throw the cow's lead rope. Birdbrain was reluctant to go, Lumpy even more reluctant. With every clumsy step the cow nearly pulled Daniel right off his horse. This would never work.

Hooves clattered behind. Was that Chet or the men? Daniel hooted low five times, a great horned owl hoot. An owl answered, pitched slightly higher. Chet! Then Tornado's black head was right by Daniel's knee. Daniel silently handed the lead line off to Chet. Chet wrapped it twice around his saddle horn and forged ahead. Daniel dropped back to where he could swat Lumpy's bony backside with the ends of his reins. He heard Llorón beside them, panting in the darkness.

Ahead of them, the moon slipped above the dry hills. Chet was twisted in the saddle, watching both before and behind. His face radiated pure joy. They had done it! Right out from under the noses of three good vaqueros!

They paused to rest by a tornillo clump. Chet loosened Tornado's cinch. The horse was sweating. Dragging a recalcitrant cow along was hard work. Chet drank from his canteen and passed it to Daniel.

"Finish it off."

Daniel did. He was thirsty and outrageously hungry. All this riding—and they faced a whole night of more riding. But they had the cow.

"Six feet," Chet whispered hoarsely. "I wasn't more than six feet from that fellow. And he didn't see me. I ain't never gonna forget that feeling, untying this cow right under his nose. Six feet, Dan. Not an inch more."

"I could never have done that. Hey, Chet. Let's pull your saddle off Tornado and put it on Birdbrain. Then I can drag the cow awhile—let Tornado rest."

"Good idea!" Chet looped his fingers into his latigo and pulled it free. He dragged the saddle off and a thin haze of steam lifted off Tornado's back. It took but a moment to saddle Birdbrain, and they were on their way again.

The moon was still high as the east got light. Daniel was so tired he did not feel tired anymore. They had switched the saddle twice more during the night, and now both horses were ready to drop. Going was so slow.

"Hey, Chet, we better rest again. Birdbrain is

94

stumbling all over the state of Texas."

"If we stop and the cow lays down, we won't get her up again."

Lumpy must have understood. She buckled her front knees. Unable to pull a kneeling cow, Tornado quit walking. Lumpy's backside folded and plopped gently to the ground.

"Chet, why'd you go and give her ideas like that?"

"Sorry. Forgot she speaks English."

"Now what do we do? We haven't come very far."

"Not far at all. Slowest cow west of the Mississippi."

Llorón curled up beside his best friend and stretched his chin out on his paws.

Daniel sighed. "We're just gonna have to leave her if those three come after us."

"Not on your life! After all we went through?"

"This old cow isn't worth dying for. Specially with you not saved."

"You mean religion? Now don't start that, Dan."

"I never preached to you."

"Good. Keep a good thing going and don't start."

Daniel opened his mouth, but he never spoke. Chet's face sent a shiver down his back. He looked behind to see what Chet was staring at in cold terror.

Three men were riding at a smart jog, coming quickly. Their horses seemed fresh and ready to go. And they were less than a mile away!

8

Pursued!

Chet was sweating, and not from heat. "They're onto us, Dan. This stupid cow isn't going to get up no matter how hard we pull and kick."

The dawn air was chilly, but Daniel was sweating too. They had done everything but build a fire under her. Lumpy would not budge.

"Chet, if she won't move for us, she won't move for them."

"They have three fresh horses. They'll pull her up."

"Well, let's not watch 'm. Come on!"

"On these horses? Take a good look at 'm, Dan."

"Will you quit contradicting everything I say and *run*?!"

Chet chewed his lip. "You're right. But on foot. *I* can outrun Tornado right now. Up in those rocks—try to work our way over the ridge without being seen. Stay low."

Chet swung off Tornado and dropped the

reins. The weary little horse let its head hang low. And Birdbrain was even worse off.

Daniel followed Chet up the steep slope. A scattering of boulders became a vast, jumble of round rocks. Here the boys would be on equal footing with their pursuers, for the men, too, would have to leave the horses behind.

The boys hopped from rock to rock until they could hear the horses below. They wedged themselves down into a cranny between two rocks and listened.

Daniel tried to keep from breathing out loud. It was hard to do. Below, the three were discussing the cow in Spanish, but their voices were too indistinct to make out. Daniel glanced at Chet. Chet was scared. Terrified.

"Did you see the Dragoon that big dude is packing?" he whispered.

"The what?"

"His gun, Dan. It can put a hole in you big enough to plant a tree. At a hundred yards."

Stones rattled below. The men had dismounted and were climbing toward them.

"Why do they want us? They have the cow."

"We can identify them."

"No we can't. I never got a look at 'm. Did you?"

"They won't believe that. All they know is, we were close enough to get the cow."

"Chet? Do you think they're gonna—uh—"

"I know they are."

Daniel grabbed Chet's sleeve. "If you die

right now, what will happen to you?"

"Shut up, Dan! I'm scared enough!"

"Chet, you're going to hell and it doesn't have to be! If they kill us right now you can go to heaven too, like me."

"You don't know that."

"I do know it, just as sure as you know what that gun can do to you. You said yesterday I never lied to you."

"I done too much wrong to get to heaven, Dan. Thanks for caring, but I—"

"Look here. If I owe Pop ten dollars, and you pay my debt for me, the debt's canceled. Doesn't matter whose money paid it. You owe God for your sins, but Jesus paid it. He didn't have to die because He didn't do any sins to die for. But He died anyway—to pay for yours. See?"

"No. How can I go to heaven when I don't understand?"

"Same as you can take a train ride without knowing how a steam engine works. But God doesn't expect you to stay dumb. Matt and I will help you learn about Him."

"A few words is all it takes, huh?"

"You have to really mean it, though. You have to be serious about following Jesus. But claim Jesus as your Savior and He'll take care of you, live or die."

Chet was shaking. He studied Daniel a few moments. "You sure? Yeah, you're sure. I want that, Dan. I want God—if He'll have me."

"Then you got Him! He promised—"

Stones rattled, closer. The men were coming up the hill on two sides. Daniel could tell just where they were.

Chet glanced around, listening. "They'll pick us off like dodos here. Bolt and run. Stay down the best you can and don't run in a straight line. We'll scatter, divide their attention."

Daniel nodded. He scanned the boulders around him, mentally picking his route. He was praying without realizing it, and his prayers were for Chet. *God, help Chet make his commitment stick. Keep Chet safe.*

Peeking between boulders, Daniel saw a sombrero float close by. Now or never. He scrambled up over the rocks to his left, bobbing from boulder to boulder. Wrong place to be! One of the three was right in front of him. The man lunged at Daniel and caught his sleeve. With a snarl, a ball of blue fury slammed into the man's chest, knocking him down. Llorón!

Daniel jerked free and started running for all he was worth.

Behind him, Llorón yelped—not in pain but in anger. He must not look back. He zigzagged, darting this way and that. A gunshot exploded behind him, and the bullet chinked into a rock a yard from his ear.

Suddenly he was down out of the rocks, and had nowhere to hide. He ran faster, like a jackrabbit, down the brush-scattered slope.

He glanced over his shoulder. The tall man was silhouetted against the clear blue sky. The man held his Dragoon in both hands, steadying his aim, zeroing in on Daniel. "At a hundred yards," Chet had said. Suddenly the man lowered his gun, turned, and disappeared into the rocks.

Horses were coming from the east, thundering down at Daniel. Were they—

They plunged past Daniel and continued toward the rock pile without faltering: Pop and Mr. Carson and Matt!

Daniel stood still a moment, too tired and too relieved to move. Then he made his weary legs start running, back to the rocks, back to Chet and the cow. He was not going to miss this!

Up ahead, Matt leaped off his horse and ran up into the boulders. Hank and Pop, the cavalry, swung wide around the rock pile. All three carried rifles, and Daniel knew all three could use them well.

Daniel reached a high spot in time to see the three rustlers gallop off into the distance, riding low and lashing their horses. Matt stood high in the rocks, his Sharps in the crook of his arm. Chet appeared near the crest and came rock-hopping slowly down the boulders.

The five met at the foot of the rock pile. Daniel melted into a rock that looked vaguely like a chair. Chet flopped on the ground beside him and stretched out.

He scratched his head, the wild, bushy red hair. "If you lumped together all the tireds I've ever been in my whole life, they wouldn't match the tired I am right now."

Pop slid off Caesar laughing, and Mr. Carson offered his two canteens around.

"How'd you three find us, Pop?"

"Matt. He tracked you here. We started out from our place soon as the moon was high enough to half see."

Chet raised his head to stare at Matt. "You tracked us by moonlight?"

"Wasn't that hard. Five horses and a cow. And a dog. I kept picking up that hound's trail here and there. He didn't come with you guys, did he?"

"On his own, later."

"Thought so."

Daniel grinned. "Not so bad for a tottery old man, eh, Chet?"

Chet grimaced, embarrassed.

Mr. Carson wagged his head. "I just took a look at that cow. I wouldn't cross the road to steal her. Or rescue her, for that matter."

Pop grinned. "Now Hank. That cow represents a capital outlay of one silver dollar. And if those three went to all this trouble, she must be worth at least that."

"Besides," said Daniel, "she's half of a set. The dog, you know. They were really trying to steal the dog."

Matt shook his head. "Not really. You see,

this eastern medical school will pay a thousand dollars for her as an example of all the things that can go wrong with a body at once."

Daniel handed the canteen back to Mr. Carson. "I know it isn't Christian, but I hate to see those three get away. Do you know one of them was shooting at me?"

Pop turned grim. "Yeah, we know. We weren't close enough to do anything about it. Couldn't shoot—might catch you in the crossfire."

"And isn't there some way we can keep Llorón? He stood up for me, jumped one of those fellows who tried to grab me."

"Me, too," said Chet. "The fat dumpy one was aiming right for me, but the hound distracted him."

"We'll talk to your Mom, Dan. Say, when that Mexican fellow saw the dog was gone, he came down to fetch him. He's at the house now, looking out for things till we get back. Nice fellow. Nothing but praise for what you did for him."

Daniel reached over and poked Chet. "Hope you remember your promise now."

"I remember."

"No backing out."

"I might do a little horse trading now and then, but I never break my word. You know what impressed me, Dan? When we were up against it there, and you didn't think about yourself. All you thought about was me. Worried about me. Nobody's ever felt that way, 'cept maybe my ma. That impressed me."

Daniel grinned. "Well, praise the Lord!"

Praise the Lord indeed! The black night, the fearsome morning drifted away. Daniel looked forward to seeing his sisters. He might even put up with "loaning" his good knife to Naomi and taking Grace's insults. He had come awfully close to losing everything. Home and everything about it looked awfully good—even chores.

Porksaddle Ridge—less than a mile from home. To sit in the warm, dark kitchen with Mom's cooking bubbling on the stove—to stretch out on his cool bed—

Pop paused on the ridgetop and scratched Lumpy behind her horns. "Let's give her another rest, Dan."

Dan sat down, and immediately Llorón lay down beside him. The big bony hound head plopped into his lap.

"Pop, I think I learned something today."

"Poor day you don't learn something. What?"

"You know how Mom makes deals with God. 'If I be good, You give me so-and-so.' And quotes Scripture."

"Yeah."

"And I suppose sometimes it works. God's nice enough to put up with it. I tried it myself.

But all the things I promised, Pop—reading the Bible and stuff—went sour. Nothing worked right. Kept getting worse, instead of better.

"But things are different now. Now I want to read the Bible and do all those things just because I want to, not so I'll earn something. I mean, it's the Bible got me through that problem with the Mexican gentleman."

"Think I've said before, the Bible's valuable."

"Yes, sir. And I want to do better by my sisters, just 'cause I want to. And Pop, it makes all the difference in the world inside me. I can feel it. You have to act like Jesus because you care. You have to read Scripture because you want to. Jesus cared, so you care. And then—"

"What Chet said this morning. What impressed him."

"Guess so. Maybe Mom can make deals, but it's not a good way. The best way is to just follow God because you care. And let Him do what's best for you because He cares."

"Yep." Pop's voice sounded a little husky. "Poor day you don't learn something." He stood up and wiped his face with his handkerchief. He picked up Lumpy's lead line and swung aboard Caesar.

"Let's go home, son."

Two strange horses were tied to the kitchen porch post. As Pop and Daniel entered the yard two strange men stepped out onto the porch.

Pop seemed to know who they were.

He stepped forward, hand out. "You're the Rangers?"

The first smiled and shook. "John Lexington, Mr. Tremain."

The second stepped forward in turn. "Henry Maddox, sir."

Mom burst out the door and paused. She did not hug Daniel in front of everybody, and he was glad. Her eyes were wet, but her voice was steady. "I'm so glad you're back safe! And you even got the cow."

Grace ran around the corner of the house and barreled into Daniel. That was not so bad. Sisters were not the same as mothers. It was wonderful, feeling cared about.

Grace hugged her father and turned to Mr. Maddox. "We saw three strange horses in the wash down behind the barn. We didn't see good. We think there's three."

Mr. Maddox smiled. "Thank you, Grace." He announced very loudly, "You folks look mighty tired. Why don't you just go inside where the coffee's hot. I'll put this little old cow away for you and be right in."

Mr. Lexington went inside. A moment later Daniel heard the front door close. Mr. Maddox led Lumpy off to the barn, her line in his left hand, his right hand lying easily on his holstered gun. Pop herded everyone inside. The kitchen door closed.

"Pop! They need help, just two of them

against those three!"

Pop shook his head. "Let 'm work. Now we find out why that blamed cow is so important."

Mom dropped into her chair. "That miserable cow! I wish I'd never set eyes on her."

Daniel robbed the cookie jar, grinning. "See, Mom? Make deals with God, and you get what you ask for."

Daniel sat down across from the Mexican gentleman and stretched out his legs. He was getting stiff. Naomi stayed in the gentleman's lap, but Rachel hopped over into Daniel's.

"Look, Dan, what Mr. Pera taught me." She pulled her bare foot up into Daniel's face. *"Este puerquito va'l mercado—este puerquito se queda en la casa."*

Daniel laughed. " 'This Little Pig' in Spanish?"

Rachel scowled. "Now I have to start over! *'Esta . . .'* "

Horses' hooves churned in the yard outside.

"Dan. Come with me." Pop headed for the door.

"Oh, Ira—" But Mom sat still.

The two rangers and their three captives were mounted and ready to go. The three were roped together neck to neck. Mr. Lexington shook his head. "Won't say a word about why they might want the cow. But we caught 'm red-handed in a rustling attempt. We'll let you know."

Pop nodded and shrugged. Everyone said

good-bye, and the riders left in a churning cloud of dust.

Pop turned to Daniel. "What are you staring at? You saw those men before."

"No, I didn't. Not up close."

"You recognize 'm?"

"Not really." But Daniel's head was swimming. That tall man with the moustache, the one who once carried the Dragoon; he was one of the two who had been fighting on that road in Mexico. Daniel started to speak but stopped. He was too tired now to think straight. He would sleep. Tomorrow he would tell Pop about the stickpin. Tomorrow for sure.

The man, the cow, the stickpin—but how—

9

Lumpy's Big Surprise

Daniel dreaded Monday morning. Mr. Devlin would not take kindly to his missing Friday. He picked at his breakfast, reluctant to make the day start happening.

Pop came in and headed for the stove. "The horses are ready. How about you kids?" He poured himself coffee, so he was obviously prepared to wait.

"Horses?" Daniel asked. "Two horses?"

"Unless you expect four people to ride on one."

"Four? Who else is going?"

"Me."

"You mean after all these years, Pop, you're gonna learn to read?"

Rachel kicked him under the table. "He can too read, silly!" She paused. "Can you, Pop?"

Pop laughed. "Thought I might go along personally and excuse your absence, since Mr. Devlin's been having problems."

"What problems?"

Grace snorted. "You know. Carrie and Barton and—"

"I wasn't there Friday, remember?"

Grace put on her casual, know-it-all face. "Mr. Devlin accused Carrie of cheating. He gave her a test she wasn't supposed to know the answers to, and she did."

"Carrie wouldn't cheat in a million years!"

Grace shrugged. "And Barton poured ink in the water bucket."

Daniel scowled. "Barrel of laughs, that Barton."

Pop drained his coffee cup. "Let's go, scholars!"

They went.

All the way to school Daniel kept wondering why Mr. Devlin would give Carrie an examination over material she was not supposed to know. But then, as he watched Pop and the teacher talking in the schoolyard, he felt perhaps he was being too critical. Mr. Devlin was all smiles and nods.

The teacher called school to order as Pop swung aboard Caesar. The little ones ran inside. Daniel dawdled a bit and entered the schoolhouse as Pop was riding out of the yard. Daniel sat down.

Mr. Devlin scowled at him. "Mr. Tremain, you may think yourself worthy of special privilege because your father made excuse for you. No such thing. See me at recess. I have work for you."

Daniel slouched down on his bench. He hated splitting kindling.

Mr. Devlin turned to Carrie. "Miss Carson, your confession?"

Carrie looked pale. She stood. "I didn't bring one."

"Surely you understood. A written confession cosigned or initialed by your parents. I want to know they are aware of your transgression."

"I didn't tell my parents, sir. Mother is ill. She gets upset very easily. And I didn't cheat, so I have nothing to confess anyway."

"Very well, you had your fair chance." Mr. Devlin's voice was cold. "You are expelled, Miss Carson." He paused, waiting. "You may take your leave."

Carrie picked up her lunch pail and books. "My conscience is clear, sir." She headed for the door.

Matt stood up.

"Yes, Matthew?"

"Sir, I don't know why you've been holding Carrie back—or Dan and Bart, for that matter—but I've been helping her keep up. If she knew the answers, I'm as much to blame as she." He started for the door, too. Daniel was itching to jump up, but he could not think of a reason to.

"Stop! Both of you!" Mr. Devlin's voice was

so sudden, so loud, that Rachel started to cry. "You claim to be seminary material, Matthew. Does either of you think I act on whim? A woman shall not teach or have authority over men, Matthew. I'm sure you've read that in Scripture. And yet you aid your sister here in contradicting Scripture. Normal school? College? Teaching is a man's work. Your sister already has more than ample education for her place as a wife and mother. Sit down."

"I see." Matthew's voice was calm, but Daniel was so angry inside his skin prickled. Matt nodded. "It was a trap, wasn't it, sir? If she flunks the test, she's not ready for eighth grade. If she passes, she must have cheated. Either way, Carrie loses. Clifton—Get your books and come."

Clifton half stood up, confused. Mr. Devlin was closer to him than Matt. Whom should he follow?

Daniel could not sit still any longer. "Grace. Rachel. Come." He stepped out into the aisle.

Mr. Devlin snatched up his ruler. "I told you all to sit down!"

Daniel grabbed Grace's wrist and yanked her toward the door. Clifton and Rachel followed her, wide-eyed. Here came Matt, grim and determined. Daniel pushed Carrie ahead of him and started walking, his back to the teacher, prepared to turn the little ones around if they had second thoughts. Now he was in the doorway, the last one out.

Mr. Devlin's ruler came down across his back, knocking him forward. He caught his balance and swung around as a brawny arm swept past his ear. The ruler went flying.

It was Chet! And now Chet was gripping Mr. Devlin's waistcoat, crushing him against the schoolhouse wall. Chet looked a foot taller than the little teacher. Mr. Devlin's feet were not even touching the ground.

"Why, howdy do, Teach!" Chet grinned. "I was coming in to talk to you 'bout Bart. See I'm just in time to show you the error of your ways. Now my friend Dan, here, would never do nothing to deserve harsh treatment—"

"Unhand me, you illiterate!"

Barton whooped in Daniel's ear. "Lay it on 'm, Chet!"

"No!" Daniel wedged himself between Chet and Mr. Devlin. The schoolmaster slid down the adobe a few inches. At least now his feet were touching ground.

Chet did not loosen up a bit. "Dan, don't you realize what he's been doing to Bart? And you and Carrie? And the Guirrans, for Pete sake! You can't be standing up for him."

"It's you I'm thinking about, Chet. You promised you were turning your life over to Jesus. The whole life. That includes this. Remember what Matt and I were saying?"

"You telling me to back off?"

"No. Jesus is. Turn the other cheek, remember?"

"He was talking about enemies. Teach, here, isn't worth the honor of being called an enemy."

Barton was still right by Daniel's ear. "My brother's gonna take you apart! You'll have so many lumps on you they'll think somebody sewed rocks in your hide!"

Chet stared at Barton a long, long moment, then turned to Mr. Devlin. "Devlin, I ain't never backed off from a fight in my whole life. Not once. And I never lost one, neither. I ain't turning you loose because you deserve it. You don't. I'm letting you go for Jesus' sake."

Chet stepped back, and the schoolmaster sagged a little. Chet swung aboard Tornado and paused. The black horse danced. "You got off scot-free this time, Devlin. But don't press your luck." He wrenched Tornado's head around and clattered away up the road.

Daniel glanced over at Matt. "It's for real!" He grinned.

Matt nodded and grinned back.

Mr. Devlin tugged his waistcoat down smooth and cleared his throat. His face, once red with anger, had turned white with fear. Now it was starting to turn red again with— embarrassment? "Come back to the school, now. All of you. Come along." He turned on his heel and disappeared inside.

Daniel glanced around. "Where's Grace?"

"She ran off as soon as she got out the door," said Carrie. "She's probably halfway home by now. Dan, you mustn't give up everything because of me, or you either, Matt. None of you. It's better that I stay home anyway, with Mom so sick. Matt can tutor me like he tutors the Guirrans."

"He what?"

Matt smiled. "You should see how fast they're learning, Dan. Every Sunday they ride over to our place, or we go over to theirs. That little Pato is especially quick. They're working awfully hard—never flub an assignment."

"Go on," soothed Carrie. "You two go back in."

Matt shook his head. "It's wrong to leave and wrong to stay. Dan, I don't know what to do."

"Well, that blows my plan." Daniel sighed.

"What plan?"

"To go along with whatever you do."

"Ah, look. Bet we don't have the choice anymore." Matt pointed down the road.

Pop was coming. Old Caesar galumphed along at a clumsy lope. Grace, her arms wrapped around Pop's waist, bounced behind him. Even from that far away they could hear her talking a mile a minute.

Pop swung his leg over Caesar's neck and slid off. "Grace, walk him out a few minutes. You little folks go play over by the trees. Barton, Matt, Carrie, Dan—come with me."

Melanie Hawes, ever nosy, started to follow.

Barton scowled at her, and she altered course for the trees.

As Pop strode through the schoolhouse door, Daniel realized what it must feel like to follow a famous general into battle. Pop said, "Sit." Everyone obediently plopped down on the nearest benches. Pop continued up to Mr. Devlin, his hand out.

Apparently Mr. Devlin did not care to shake hands just then. He sat behind his desk. "Mr. Tremain, I was told when I accepted this position that I would teach without interference. We made specific agreement to that effect."

"You can't teach an empty schoolroom, sir."

"I see you're not going to just leave politely. Very well. You children, out. Go." Mr. Devlin looked grim, even fearful.

No one moved.

"They aren't children, Mr. Devlin. Every boy here does a man's work. Carrie has the responsibility for her household with her mother being ill. They're old enough to do a grown person's work—they're old enough to hear what we say."

Daniel's cheeks warmed with pride.

"And besides, they have some tall explaining to do. Some apologies, too, I wager."

Daniel's cheeks cooled off immediately.

Mr. Devlin stood up. "I see. I did not speak lightly, Mr. Tremain. I couch no interference. You will have my resignation in the morning. Good day." He circled his desk and started walking toward the door.

It was so smooth—Pop had Mr. Devlin's elbow and had steered the teacher to a bench before he knew what happened. Pop sat him down and sat down across from him, eye to eye. Daniel had not noticed until today—comparing Chet and now Pop—how short Mr. Devlin really was.

"Mr. Devlin, I always thought it strange that a good schoolmaster should be clerking in a store. I take it you've had trouble like this before, or you wouldn't have mentioned that no-interference business."

Judging by the way Mr. Devlin stiffened, that must be it!

"If you insist on resigning, I can't stop you. But I can urge you not to. The Lord gave you a gift for teaching little ones. My Rachel is halfway through her first reader and ciphering fine. Hank has nothing but good words about Clifton's progress. We need you. I can't promise you no problems, but I can promise these boys will behave."

"I don't need an outsider to handle my discipline for me."

"If I were in your shoes I sure would. Ten kids in eight grades is too heavy a load for one man to balance. Hank Carson will be in to talk to you about Carrie. Until then, Carrie, I suggest going home early will just upset your mother. You might hang around here and go home with Matt and Cliff this afternoon. Let your father handle it, not Clara."

Carrie nodded, still very sad.

Pop continued, "Barton, come'ere."

Barton hopped up, nervous.

"Bart, you been acting like a ninny ever since first grade. You need the book learning. An ignorant man gets taken advantage of, and you'll soon be a man. You already do a man's work, so start acting like one. Any more hot tricks and you answer to me. And don't expect Chet to do your fighting for you. I can floor him, too, if I have to. Now what do you say to Mr. Devlin?"

Barton's shoulders sagged. He mumbled something.

"Louder. To him."

"Sorry about the ink. I mean the water bucket."

"Which reader you in, Barton?"

"Fourth."

"I expect you to be in the fifth by month's end, so you better get working. Dan, what reader you in?"

"Third."

Pop's head snapped back. "Why didn't you say something before this?"

"I was gonna—"

Pop studied Mr. Devlin.

"As you say," said the teacher, "ten children is a heavy load. I hadn't found the time to examine him yet." His eyes were darting about; the worried look was still all over his face.

Mr. Devlin started talking again about no interference, but Daniel was not listening. He was watching Pop. Pop was thinking; you could tell by the thin line his mouth made. Suddenly he interrupted Mr. Devlin. "These boys are all bigger than you, even Daniel. Any one of them could pick you up. You wouldn't be afraid of them, sort of."

"Nonsense!"

"All right, uneasy then. Uncomfortable. So you've been passing them over and working with the little ones."

"If that were true, Matthew wouldn't be so far advanced."

"Matt's the exception. You'd be proud to turn out a seminary candidate. These other farmers, that's another thing. Right? Well, you get them promoted up and out, and they'll be out of your hair. Push 'm. Make 'm work! And I guarantee they'll cooperate." Pop stood up. "Good to talk to you, Mr. Devlin."

Daniel stood up, too. "Pop. I think I'd rather stay outside with Carrie."

Matthew stood up. "Me, too, sir."

Pop considered a moment. "What'd you do when you found our cow was stolen?"

Daniel shrugged. "Went after it."

"Didn't run away from the problem?"

Daniel caught Pop's line of thought right away. He sighed. "No, sir."

"You acted. Had a problem and acted. I admit that problem was more straightforward

119

than this one. Easier to see. But you'll not solve this one or any other by walking out. You'll stay and you'll help Mr. Devlin be the best teacher he can be."

"But you don't understand—"

"Answers aren't always easy. And seldom perfect. Do your best and leave the wrinkles for God to iron out."

"Yes, sir." Daniel sat down.

"And no more rebellion in the ranks."

"No, sir."

Pop nodded. "God bless you, Mr. Devlin." And he walked outside.

The children clustering in the doorway filed silently back to their benches. Mr. Devlin sat quietly at his desk again. Daniel expected him to explode, like fireworks.

"I—I need time to think. School is dismissed until tomorrow morning. Go. All of you." His head dropped into his hands.

The little kids were totally confused. Grace hurried out to catch Pop. The Hawes girls left, then the rest trickled out. The room was deadly quiet.

Daniel looked at Matt. Matt did not know what to say, but it seemed something ought to be said.

Daniel shuffled his feet a moment. "Jesus loves you, Mr. Devlin."

No response.

The boys stepped outside. Daniel closed the door behind him.

The ride home—Pop on Caesar with Rachel up behind, Daniel on Cleopatra with Grace—was dismally quiet. It was not just school, which was bleak enough. Had Mr. Pera left, taking Llorón with him? What about the cow? Maybe someone else would try to steal her. And the stickpin—he could not tell Pop about the stickpin now. Everything that went into the girls' ears came out their mouths.

As they approached the house, Daniel saw Mr. Pera standing by the corner of the yard, watching. The blue-speckled hen strutted out into the road. Suddenly, Llorón came bounding out. The hen squawked and flapped, but she was not fast enough.

"Oh, no!" screamed Daniel and Grace together. Mr. Pera did not move.

Llorón grabbed the hen by her back. Suddenly he yelped. He howled. The hen went fluttering off, forgotten. Llorón rubbed his head in the dirt and ran in little circles, yelping.

Pop grinned at Mr. Pera. Mr. Pera grinned back.

Pop smiled. "So it worked. He won't chase chickens anymore, I bet."

"What worked?" Daniel asked.

"Kerosene and hot pepper. Mr. Pera's idea. You just touch a little bit around on the feathers. Gets in the dog's mouth."

Daniel grabbed his father's arm. "Does that mean we can keep Llorón?"

"Yep. Your Mom and I talked it over. The

121

chickens was the only problem, and Mr. Pera just solved that."

"Yahoo!" Grace slid off Cleopatra's rump and ran for the house, to be there first with all the news. She came right back out, confused. "Mom isn't there."

Pop called, "Martha?"

From the barn came her muffled voice. "In here."

Daniel entered the barn right behind Pop. "What is that terrible smell?"

"I know what, but I sure don't know why. Martha, what in blazes are you doing in here with—whiskey—mash." Pop's voice trailed off to nothing.

Daniel came up beside him and peeked over the top rail of the cow's stall. The stall was just full of the bad smell. Mom held a basin of the vilest gruel Daniel had ever seen. And there was Chet, sitting on the milk stool beside the cow. He was stitching up a long, gaping cut with Mom's darning needle. The cut, and another just like it, were all that was left of the two abcesses in Lumpy's flank.

Pop wagged his head. "I don't get it."

Mom was so excited she was trembly. "Chet thought of it. He came over an hour ago."

Chet knotted the last stitch and broke the thread. "Hit's Barton who gave me the idea. Remember, Dan? He said something about sewing rocks up in your hide."

"Yeah, but—"

"How about rocks like diamonds and emeralds?"

Mom set aside the basin and picked up two rancid, soiled cotton sacks by her feet. "Look, Ira! The Carlota settings! Those weren't abscesses, they were these!"

Even as filthy as they were, the jewels were beautiful.

"Clever!" said Pop. "That kind of thing would kill a horse. But you could slip them under a cow's skin, and no problem. Bring the cow north across the border—just an old cow. Nothing suspicious. But she broke away or wandered off somewhere."

Chet chimed in. "And the smugglers heard somehow that Mr. Pera had an old tan cow. He says he found her wandering around loose."

"And when he didn't have her any more, they must have been madder'n hornets!" Daniel added. "That's why they—Can you imagine how frustrated they must have been? All those jewels on the hoof, wandering around, lost—Uh, lost. I'll be right back!"

Daniel raced to the house and up into the loft. He fished out the rolled-up socks. There it was. He ran back to the barn. "You know that tall one, the fellow with the Dragoon? I saw him before, Pop, in Mexico. He fought with a man, and right afterwards I found this on the ground."

Pop twisted it this way and that to make the

jewels gleam. "And you think he dropped this."

"It looks that way now. Sorry, Mom. That was gonna be your Christmas present."

Mom was wagging her head. "I can't believe all this. It's just too—Why, Rachel! Why are you crying, honey?"

"Chet hurt her. He hurt Lumpy cutting her."

"She'll feel so much better now that those sacks are out from under her skin, dear."

Chet put away his knife and dropped down to eye level with Rachel. "Rachel, girl, your old Lumpy didn't feel a thing. Since I made a promise to God, I busted up my whiskey still. This here's the mash that was left. Eight gallons of useless whiskey mash. So we used it to get Lumpy, uh, tipsy."

"Tipsy?"

Mom picked Rachel up. "Honey, Lumpy didn't feel a solitary thing. Feeling no pain, as the saying goes."

Pop rubbed his hands together. "Guess I'll ride into Springer and wire Mr. Lexington again. Looks like the whole thing is cleared up, thanks to you boys."

"Only one little problem, Pop. Now we don't have anything for Mom for Christmas."

Chet laughed. "You know how much reward you're gonna get for this stuff, Dan?"

"No. Do you?"

"Not exactly, but I guarantee you this: You

don't have to worry about no Christmas present."

Lumpy mooed a silly, bugling moo and took a step toward the mash basin. She almost fell over.

Mom laughed. "Sorry, Lumpy! This stuff gets buried. You've had the last of it. You're on the wagon."

Outside, a hen squawked—it sounded like one of the red ones. Immediately, a plaintive hound's voice yelped and wailed. Above the whining, the red hen's voice clucked and scolded across the yard.

Daniel looked at Pop and shrugged. "He learns a little slow sometimes."

Pop grinned. "Stupid old melon hound."

Moody Press, a ministry of the Moody Bible Institute, is designed for education, evangelization, and edification. If we may assist you in knowing more about Christ and the Christian life, please write us without obligation: Moody Press, c/o MLM, Chicago, Illinois 60610.